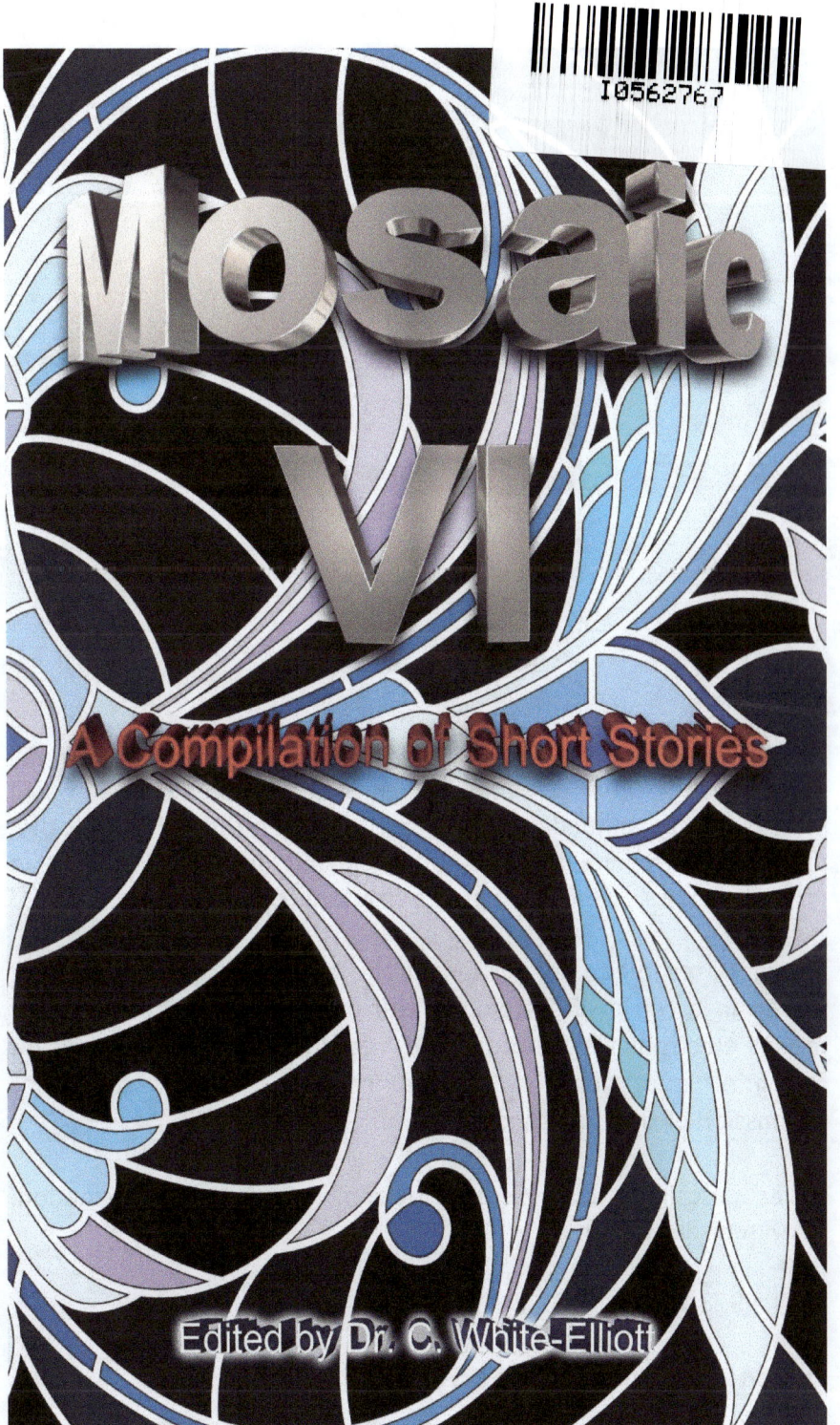

MoSaic

VI

A Compilation of Short Stories

Edited by Dr. C. White-Elliott

This book contains works of both non-fiction and fiction. In the cases of fictional writings, the stories may have been fashioned after true stories but are not exact retellings.

CLF Publishing, LLC.
www.clfpublishing.org

Cover design by Senir Design. Contact information: info@senirdesign.com.

ISBN # 978-1-945102-31-8

Printed in the United States of America.

Dedications

This book is dedicated to all aspiring writers who were told they couldn't make it in the field of writing or who may have been too scared to move forward because of a fear of failure.

The writers, whose stories are included within, are proof that you can be successful and your dreams can be a reality.

So, I invite you to pursue your own writing and be the success you know you are.

Dr. Cassundra White-Elliott

Acknowledgements

I acknowledge all the participants in this project, who helped to see it from its stages of inception to its complete fruition.

May your success be plentiful, as you continue to pursue your educational and writing endeavors. I look forward to working with each of you individually, collectively, or both, in the near future.

Much love and appreciation,

C. White-Elliott

Dr. Cassundra White-Elliott

Table of Contents

Introduction

Welcome to **The Mosaic**, where you will enter the exciting world of short stories. Here, the imagination can and will unfold right before your very eyes. What you least expect just may become the expected.

The fourteen authors have delved within their own imaginations and pulled out all the stops and barred no holds. Their tales will excite you, cause curiosity to grow, bring tears of sadness, and/or even feelings of wonderment.

They are skillful in their craft, and they are to be congratulated for their efforts. They have stepped into unknown territory with publishing and sharing their talents with the world at large.

So, I invite you to sit back, relax with your favorite drink, curl up in your most comfortable chair and be prepared for the journeys that lie ahead.

With no further ado, I invite you to ENJOY!!!!!!!!!!

Little Lolly

Demian Dimmae

A Life Lost

A child lost and all alone, I had no voice
A child forced upon, I had no choice
My mom didn't hear me, nor did she see me
My dad the boogie man, used and abused me
Courage drained from my inner soul
Allowed fear to creep in and take a hold
Leaving behind tattered and torn
A life lost, a life to morn.

Demian Dimmae

It was a cold blistering Christmas Eve in New Jersey. The ground was covered with fresh powdered snow from the two-day snow storm that kept most people buried inside. It seemed no one wanted to venture out, except us kids. Not many cars were on the road. I guess it was because when it got that cold, cars didn't start so well, which meant One Mile Road would be blocked off for sledding.

It was Sissy who called me early that morning to meet up with her and Boobie at the corner candy store. From there, we would walk to Little Lolly's house. Boobie told Sissy that Little Lolly didn't want to go with us. Little Lolly had been acting strangely the last couple of months. She had become very quiet. We knew something was wrong because she started becoming more and more withdrawn and weird acting. We just didn't know what was making her act that way. She would cry or get quiet when we asked her what was wrong. Our plan was to snap her out of it and surprise her by showing up at her house with candy and bribe her to hang out with us like old times. We figured our candy bribe and begging her would make her give in. We knew how much she liked candy. We also knew how competitive she was, and the mere thought of one of us beating her speed race record down One Mile Road would force her to hang out.

I was so excited to see my friends and go sledding after days of being trapped inside the snow-bound house. I had been trapped inside for two days, doing nothing but watching the snow fall. I thought the endless flakes would never end. The only good thing about being trapped inside was I wasn't inside a classroom. School was out for Christmas vacation. Yay!

That morning, I hurried and ate breakfast, got dressed, and dug my sleigh out of the cellar where it had been since last winter. That was the first big snow we kids had been waiting for. It seemed as though it would never come. During the winter season, going sledding with my friends was what I looked forward to. It was the next best thing to opening all my Christmas gifts, and yes, it was finally Christmas Eve.

I hurried off to meet my friends with my paint-chipped sled dragging behind me. When I got there, Boobie was eagerly waiting, and Sissy was not too far behind me. We heard her calling out our names. We began to run towards each other laughing all the way. We gave big hugs, and off we went, each dragging behind us worn but well-maintained sleds. We all eagerly went in to buy Little Lolly's favorite candy; then, off we went to Little Lolly's house. The closer we got we could see Little Lolly in the distance behind the row housing complex next to a field of trees. We wanted to run toward her, but the snow was so deep we were up to our knees. We thought she was on her way to meet and surprise us at the candy store. But, she wasn't moving toward us.

As we edged closer, we saw her standing over a smoking trash can, not moving at all, but frozen solid. We called out to her, but she didn't look our way. We all said together, "She can't hear us." But the closer we got to her, we could see the smoke bellowing from the old rusty trash can that sat next to the old oak tree behind Ms. Ida's row house. We saw Little Lolly staring as the smoke drifted into the gray sky. She stayed frozen as though she were a mannequin in a department store. The look on her face was a mixture of shock and fear as she heard us call out her name. But instead of beckoning us over, she ran away, leaving the three of us to wonder why.

It was unusual for her to do that because we had dubbed ourselves as the Four Musketeers. Sissy, age eleven, was the chubby one; Boobie, age nine, was the baby of the group; I, age ten, was the tall one; and Little Lolly, age eleven, was the short one. We were the best of friends. Everything we did, we did together. We cut our fingers and became blood sisters. We took an oath to always keep each other's secrets and never lie to each other. We knew everything about each other, or so we thought.

So what could be the reason for Little Lolly to run from us? Naturally, we couldn't wait to see what was burning that made her run away. As we began to rush over to the smoldering trash can, we were stopped by Ms. Ida, better known as the town gossip, rushing out her back door while screaming at us, saying we started a fire. Her voice kept getting louder and louder, accusing us of trying to burn her house down. The whole neighborhood was convinced that she did not like kids that much. She brought with her a dish pan of water, dripping all the way. Before we could explain we had nothing to do with the thick dark smoke seeping out the trash can, she threw water on it.

As the smoke settled, she glanced in the trash can, which now was covered with burnt black soot from the smoke. Suddenly, she had the same look on her face as Little Lolly did. She began to back up, while holding her stomach and shaking her head. Her mouth was moving, but only unrecognizable sounds muttered out. She turned to look at us and became frozen as Little Lolly did. Her eyes were big, and her mouth was open, as she turned and stared at the three of us with a horrified look on her face.

I moved back, and my friends gathered close to me. We began asking, "What is wrong? Why are you looking at us like that?" We insisted we did not start the fire. But, she was frozen for a long time, for what seemed like an eternity. I kept fighting back tears. I knew if she told my mom, my mom would believe her. That is what parents did in the 1960's, believed what the old folks said. I looked at Sissy who then was backing up more and more. Boobie began pulling me by the hand in a gesture to go. I noticed her hand was shaking. I didn't budge. I knew if I did, the story Ms. Ida would tell could cause me not to get my Christmas gifts waiting for me under the tree at home.

I was determined to convince her that we had not started the fire and did not know who did. That would have been a lie, but I wasn't going to tell on my blood sister. So, I kept defending against her words, explaining we had nothing to do with the fire. Ms. Ida suddenly snapped out of her daze and interrupted me and said in a low, slow yet stern voice, "What did you kids do?" Boobie, Sissy, and I looked at each other shaking our heads to signify nothing, as we grew more and more frightened. What was running through my mind was what could be in the trashcan that would cause her and Little Lolly to have the same horrified look on their faces.

I couldn't believe what was happening. It was Christmas Eve, and our plan to go sledding on One Mile Road, which was the steepest hill in town, was about to go awry. All the kids were going to be there. We were supposed to be on our way to a good time. But from the way things were going, it didn't look like that was going to happen. I too wanted to run for dear life. But I guess Ms. Ida saw the terror in my eyes and reached to grab my arm. I moved quickly and said, "I don't want you to touch me. I didn't do anything. You're trying to get me in trouble."

My voice grew louder and turned to screaming at her and talking back, causing the others to begin to scream at her until Mr. Reed, in the house next door, came running to our rescue. As he approached us, my friends and I started to tell what was Ms. Ida was trying to accuse us of. Of course nothing we said could be understood with all of us talking at once. It wasn't until Ms. Ida screamed, "Shut up, you bad kids," that we quieted down, still defending ourselves against her accusations. Mr. Reed asked her, "What in Sam Hell is going on, and why are there ashes on the ground?" They had flown out when Ms. Ida threw water in the trashcan.

We began to speak all at once, and Ms. Ida butted in and said we did a horrible thing and he should call the police. He looked at her in amazement and told her kids will be kids, and it should not be a matter for the police. She told him to look in the trashcan. He walked over, peered in, and slowly stepped back. The color seemed to drain from his face, and he told us how horrible we were, and that we were going to jail for what we had done. He made us stand there, us shaking from fear not cold. I couldn't have felt the cold if I wanted to. I was numb from pure fear of going to jail. That made me more afraid than what my mom would do to me.

Mr. Reed told Sissy to go with Ms. Ida to make the calls to the police and our parents. Sissy was crying so hard she could hardly walk. I stood there begging Mr. Reed to listen to us. Boobie tried to go over and look in the trashcan to see what we were being accused of. She must have been thinking the same thing I was. What could be in the trash that would make them go so crazy and call the police? As she was about to look in, he shouted, "Don't you dare! You don't need to look now. You know what you kids did." Ms. Ida had disappeared into the house with Sissy heavily sobbing.

They emerged from the house a few minutes later, with Sissy crying even harder. A dozen or so people came because they heard the police sirens. The closer the police car got to us, I began to cry. I was so scared. Ms. Ida and Mr. Reed signaled for the policeman to come to them. We watched his eyes get big the more they talked. They whispered so softly I couldn't hear a thing. That scared me more than I already was. I thought when the police arrived, we would finally know what we were being accused of burning.

When I saw my mom, I rushed over and threw my arms around her professing our innocence. I was holding her so tightly she was barely able to move. Ms. Ida had Sissy by the hand to prevent her from running away, which she probably would have. She stated that Boobies' parents couldn't be reached, but a message had been left where they worked. Finally, Sissy's dad showed up with an angry and concerned look and immediately began asking questions. Sissy broke away from Ms Ida's grasp, ran, and hid behind him, saying nothing. Boobie was left without anyone, and I signaled for her to come over to me. She eased over as though she was trying not to be seen. But seen we were. We were the targets of all the commotion.

As the policeman beckoned for my mom and Sissy's dad to come over to where Ms. Ida and Mr. Reed were hunched over the now smokeless trashcan pointing down, we kids were told to stay behind. While we three blood sisters stood there trying to figure out what Little Lolly had done, we became more and more terrified of the unknown. We looked at each other, and we all seemed to know what we needed to do. When we saw that look on the policeman's face, we knew we had some explaining to do. But what could we explain when didn't have a clue of what they were looking at.

Mom walked towards me and told me to go home. Sissy was told the same thing. Boobie asked if she could go with one of us and was told no. She asked why and was told because the police didn't want us to talk to each other and that her mom left word she was on her way to get her. We each just looked at each other, crying and wondering what was going to happen to us. We didn't have a chance to make a plan if we would tell on Little Lolly. We didn't have chance to make any plans. I guess that was the plan, just not ours. I hoped Sissy and Boobie would do the same thing I knew I was, just tell the truth. That was the only way we wouldn't be blamed for whatever was so frightening in the trashcan.

Mom finally came home and asked me a lot of questions. Soon after, Daddy came home and asked me the same questions, but with much less sweetness. I told them the truth. An hour or so later, after I had been drilled by Mom and Daddy, the police came to my house to question me. My mom and dad were protectively by my side. The policeman had another policeman with him. They both asked me a series of questions, and I had no choice but to tell them the truth. I told them how we saw Little Lolly behind Ms. Ida's house with the tall oak tree next to the field staring at the smoking trashcan, and that she ran when called her. I told them we went over to see what she was staring at, but before we got there, Ms. Ida stopped us and accused us of starting a fire to burn her house down.

They listened, wrote a lot and said they would be in touch with my parents. As soon as they left, I called Boobie and Sissy and found out they told the truth as well, probably because they were told to tell the truth by their parents and were afraid as I was about what would happen if they lied. It wasn't until we went back to school that not just us kids, but all the kids in the neighborhood found out what was burning in the trashcan.

What was burning consumed the whole town's conversations. The gossip was like a dark cloud, a shadow that followed me, my friends, and, I guess, all the kids who lived in that town. The parents were so afraid that one of us would end up doing something so despicable as what they said Little Lolly had done. Who would have guessed Little Lolly had burned her dead premature newborn baby in the trash, so no one would know she had given birth? She might have gotten away with it, if we had not seen her in the far distance, and she had not run away but to us, which made us curious. If she had only ran to meet us, we would have believed whatever she said she was doing and proceeded with our plan to go sledding.

The chain of events would have never happened. Ms. Ida would have never been the wiser. The trash would have been picked up by the dump truck. We would have had a great time that day sledding and doing what we did best, be kids. Surprisingly, nothing happened to Little Lolly. I guess it was a different time and people in a back country small town went unpunished, or so we thought, especially when they felt sorry for what had been happening to Little Lolly.

For years, she had been molested since she was five years old, yet she never said a word to us, or anyone for that matter. However, what she was dealing with explains why she had changed so much in her appearance. Her mother, months later, admitted that she had suspected something, but was in denial. Little Lolly's dad had gotten wind of what Little Lolly had done and disappeared. He was later found and arrested, but the talk continued, and we lost our blood sister when her mom moved and took Little Lolly away. We thought we would see her some place, maybe the next town over, or when shopping in the nearby city, but we never did. Christmas that year was supposed to be the best ever, but it felt more like a Halloween nightmare.

It took months before the towns' people stopped talking about it. In time, it died like most stories did in towns where life was slow, with nothing to do and the highlight was to gossip. That is what we kids thought anyway: that old people worried too much about everyone's business and not enough about their own. If they had not continued to talk for months and months, maybe Little Lolly's mom wouldn't have taken her away. The moral to this true story, for me, is simple: Mind your own business, gossip less, and do the right thing. That's the silver lining to this story.

About the Author

Demian Dimmae writes poetry and short stories about women in various situations. She tries to reach the readers by pulling them in and taking them on an emotional journey. Her literature provides a short glimpse of the ups and downs around drama, trauma, and sometimes the pleasures that women encounter at one time or another. All her literary works are meant to be conversation pieces. Her goal is to open eyes and hearts to allow for healing.

Walk to the Store

Kimberly Enriquez

The Abduction
Stanley Kunitz, 1905 - 2006

Some things I do not profess to understand, perhaps
not wanting to, including whatever it was they did
with you or you with them that timeless summer day
when you stumbled out of the wood, distracted, with your white
blouse torn and a bloodstain on your skirt.
"Do you believe?" you asked. Between us, through the years,
we pieced enough together to make the story real:
how you encountered on the path a pack of sleek, grey hounds,
trailed by a dumbshow retinue in leather shrouds; and how
you were led, through leafy ways, into the presence of a royal stag,
flaming in his chestnut coat, who kneeled on a swale of moss
before you; and how you were borne aloft in triumph through the
green, stretched on his rack of budding horn,
till suddenly you found yourself alone in a trampled clearing.

That was a long time ago, almost another age, but even now,
when I hold you in my arms, I wonder where you are.
Sometimes I wake to hear the engines of the night thrumming
outside the east bay window on the lawn spreading to the rose
garden.
You lie beside me in elegant repose, a hint of transport hovering on
your lips,
indifferent to the harsh green flares that swivel through the room,
searchlights controlled by unseen hands. Out there is a childhood
country,
bleached faces peering in with coals for eyes.
Our lives are spinning out from world to world;
the shapes of things are shifting in the wind.
What do we know beyond the rapture and the dread?

My name is Crystal Page. I am twelve years old. I was abducted at the age of ten in the year 1983, in a small town called Preston. Its population is consistently around five thousand. I was a young joyous girl with brown wavy locks, blue eyes as clear as the sea, skin white as snow, and freckles that ran across my cheekbones and forehead. I was always the type of child to run around and play ball outside in the hottest, sunniest or coldest, freezing, winters. I mostly played football with the boys instead of playing volleyball with the girls like I should have been. I loved to compete, and I didn't mind a nudge here and there. I wasn't afraid of the weather, sports, or boys. I wasn't afraid of anything.

Every afternoon, I would go to the lofty market for a little stroll to buy some of my favorite junk food, which included rainbow Skittles, hot Cheetos, and ice cold Coca Cola. My parents always permitted me go to the store on my own. It was at the corner of the block. They thought because it was so close nothing could ever happen to me; plus, I never wandered off. But as I didn't know and they didn't know, someone had been watching me for the last two weeks.

He would watch me during the times I would play outside and the times I would go to the lofty market. He calculated and planned everything to avoid getting caught. To be more specific, he found a way to reel me in. I knew who this man was; he was no stranger to me. It was my neighbor forty-two year old Don Jefferson. He lived across the street from us, just a few houses down. I would rarely see him outside. The only times I did see him was when he would trim or water his plants and perhaps pick up his mail.

Don wasn't the type of person you would see caroling on Christmas or handing out candy on Halloween. He always kept to himself. He was always quite odd. He had short brown hair that never grew out, and he dressed with casual faded jeans, a long sleeve shirt and a knit sweater. He wore the same style as always, no matter how the weather was. It was his signature look. Little did I know, this man would be the one take to my childhood, joy and air.

I was headed to the store on one hot windy afternoon when the red horizon had hit earth and the sky had pasted its mood. The air was crisp and hot, blowing my hair to the sides. No cars were heard, not even a bird's simplest chirp. Only my lazy steps were heard dragging across the pavement floor. I remember I felt uneasy that day with every step I took the closer I got to the store. I had asked myself why did I feel so melancholy. Maybe I just needed my junk food to cheer me up. That always got me into a good mood.

I walked a few more steps, and I was there at the lofty market. I got my junk food, greeted the clerk lady Jessy as always, and paid. Then, I was on my way home. However, as I walked out, something unfamiliar happened. My neighbor Don was outside the store. I flashed him my white bright smile and continued to walk home. But as I was walking, he walked by my side. I was on the sidewalk, and he was at the edge of the road. He didn't seem mind and started to converse.

Don made quick but fascinating talk about these new born three-month-old brown Labrador puppies his sister had given him for his birthday. He wanted me to see them, but I knew it wasn't the right time, and I had to head home. However, he kept bragging about how cute, tiny, and fluffy they were. He said he was thinking of giving me one as well. He figured since I was his neighbor, he might as well give me one because he didn't want all those puppies to himself. I thought about it a while and decided what the heck I might as well see them. They were just puppies; my parents would understand. I was really anxious to see the Labrador puppies. I couldn't help but smile at the mention of him wanting to give me one to. I am a big animal lover. I had three cats, three dogs, eight chickens, and a hamster. I couldn't doubt that he knew that too.

He then convinced me with the nonstop detail of the pupples. I couldn't resist any longer. At that point in the conversation, he had asked me once again if I wanted to go see them. I nodded my head in agreement. As we crossed the empty street, I looked up curiously at him and noticed he had a weird crooked smile running across his chapped lips. I just thought perhaps he didn't have the best smile, but he was trying to be friendly. Who would have known within a few minutes I would know his true intentions and reality would hit me hard in the face.

He opened the door for me. As I walked in, a strong smell of cigarettes and bacon brushed against my nose. It was a smell I wasn't familiar with. My house always smelled like fresh roses or women's perfume. I walked further into the house. It was pretty neat and organized. Picture frames hanged against the walls, furniture at its place, and there was a new wood floor, as it seemed. Besides the smell of the cigarettes, the house seemed fine, just like any other American house. Strangely, I didn't hear any whimpers, smell or any view of the puppies.

Then, I turned and asked him confusingly, "Sir, where are the puppies?" He looked down at me and flashed his crooked smile again and said, "Dear, there were no puppies in the first place."

At first, my mind didn't recollect what he had just told me. My head was spinning. I didn't understand what was going on or what was going to happen to me. But as my world started spinning, he began to walk towards me. I tried to run, but I stumbled and fell hopelessly against the wooden floor. He picked me up and started walking down to the basement. As he walked steadily down the stairs, he caressed my face. I kicked and screamed and even tried punching him, but nobody could have heard my desperate cries, and I knew it too well after every lower step he too to the basement. I had no idea how I was going to get out of there.

As I frantically tried to scramble out of his arms, he looked and me and said, "You're mine." I cried and cried. I couldn't stop. Then, we had finally made it to the shadowed dark basement. That afternoon, my innocence was taken away.

It has been two sad long years that I have been locked up in his basement. I don't understand how they didn't see Don as a possible suspect. I spent sunrise after sunrise and shining moonlight after moonlight there. Every single one of them I had missed because of this dreadful dark basement.

I wonder everyday how my family is doing or what they think has happened to me. Do they think I died, ran away or disappeared? If only they knew that I am still here. Their baby girl is hanging on and waiting for them to find her. I never give up hope for the day I get out of this jail of a basement to once again feel the hot sun's heat soaking into my pores and to be able to see the moonlight and its little brothers and sisters the stars and to once again run and play ball in the streets in the winter days.

I never give up hope. I never will. How am I? Crystal Page...

About the Author

Kimberly Enriquez was nineteen years old and a freshman at College of the Desert at the time she penned this story. She tends to persuade the major of Psychology. She lives in a small town called Salton City and lives three miles away from the lake. Sometimes, she likes to walk around there for a peaceful and tranquil time, with just herself, the lake, and the air.

In her free time, she loves to watch movies or just sit in her room and listen to music. She's a calm girl, who doesn't go out, and she really can't go out because Salton City is a small place where there isn't much to do. There's only desert and the lake, but that's the beauty of it. There's no noise or disturbances.

Changing Tides

Raena Fisk

Escape

The sun shines down on the vineyards

Another day

Grapes are pungent in the heat

Like a wet dog in summer

The valley is beautiful

But I've been here too long

It's time to more on

Visit new places

See unfamiliar faces

Just for one day

~Raena Fisk

Looking up, I see the waning gibbous moon illuminating the sand. Picking up a palmful reveals that it's damp and holds together well. I try to sit and shield myself from the biting wind blowing off the top of my sand dune and succeed, reminding myself of the same wind that whips across my face when I ride my bike to school in the morning. Behind me, the Pacific Ocean roars. I am completely and utterly alone.

I remember my first road trip to Dillon Beach, California. It was almost nine years ago, when I was young enough to still think I knew everything about the world. At the time, it was my kingdom, and I was the queen of it all, from Tomales Point to the northern tip of Bodega Bay. It was a place of happiness and serenity, and as I got older, it became the place where I went to leave my hectic world of reality behind to escape to the freedom of the sea and salt. This time, however, my feeling of ecstasy is heavily tainted with a sense of loss, or that something (or someone) is missing. It's ironic, seeing how I always come out here to feel complete.

Another gust of wind slaps me in the face, and I decide to move away from the choppy airspace at the top of the dune. Walking down to the pebbly beach, I wonder why I chose to come here at this time of day, or rather, night. But then again, I think to myself, it's worth it just to be out here once more.

Continuing up the shore, I stagger slightly from the wind and yearn to be inside the little cafe at the entrance to the small beach town that is Dillon Beach, with a gigantic mug of their incomparable hot chocolate. My hood refuses to cooperate and keeps being blown off my head. The tiny flashlight in my mouth is my only beacon, but I turn it off and let the moonlight guide me. This entire time I am unable to think of anything but the cold. Combined with the shadows of the cliffs and jagged rocks that line the surf, it makes me think that something is watching me, that my demons have tracked me here. I'm confused as to why this place is giving me these feelings of unease. Why has my childhood safe haven morphed into such a hostile environment?

My footsteps crumble the sand beneath me, as if to mock my attempt to depart from civilization and lay down a bright, shining path for my demons to follow. The jagged slab of granite I now sit on reminds me of said demons, Unease and Crisis, along with their daughter Sorrow. Unwanted recollections are forced to the front of my mind: a prank gone horribly wrong, a friendship torn apart, and a year of painful regret.

I now remember why I haven't come back in so many months. A scene begins to unfold before my eyes, taking shape and reality as a whip-like strand of brown seaweed flashes in front of me. An unmistakable *crack* reverberates inside my skull. A young girl screams and drops to her knees before me, her hands over her face as her fingers begin to leak, a trickle of rust at first but quickly becoming a deep, rich crimson. I observe her, confused by her anguish, until I look down at my own hands to see the tool of her despair resting in my palm. The scene swirls, obscured by my unconscious trying to block it out completely but not before my own wail of realization echoes through my mind. I shake my head.

Is there no end to the violence? I have no choice but to carry on off the rock and up the beach, searching for some point of relief while getting nothing but another smack of airborne ice to my features and fingers. My extremities are numb. My mind is clogged with harsh thoughts of the past. My once great kingdom has turned to evil and despair.

My haven has become a frigid hell.

I look for an escape, some bush or boulder that can spare me from this cold, bitter land. I journey onward, willing myself to keep going and persevere. Now with each slap from the gusts of wind comes a distinct and strong scent of salt and brine. I continue walking, dodging the surges of the incoming tide, until I come to a graveyard of giant boulders and cliff points. It is my final destination, and my reason for slugging through the desolate waste that was once my oceanside empire.

I start on the south end, knowing that the object I search for is there. My flashlight beams over every stone and pebble in vain, as it reveals nothing. I search the north end as well despite my logical judgment, taking an extremely close look at every rock that could possibly be the one, but come up with nothing. Accepting defeat, I turn back down the beach, only to spot a most familiar shape in front of me.

My serpentine. Or rather, my father's, for he has always said that he'd relocate it to our front yard someday. There it is, all two tons of it, its emerald sheen reflecting the moonlight in between its milky white streaks of quartz. The serpentine boulder was once a decorative piece in the backyard of one of the houses on the cliffs above me but had long since fallen to sea level when the cliff had eroded away. It's a familiar figure, a constant, ever-present entity that I always visit out here. The sight of it brings me relief, for not all in my kingdom has changed.

Suddenly, the beach calls a truce. The hostility ends. The

wind is nothing but a salty breeze to me now. The sea is a sleepy but joyful hum of peace, and I have literally found my rock.

I hear a car horn in the distance. Quickly, I pat the rock that has become such a part of me as the beach has and turn back to walk the way I came. As I reach the foot of the path to the small grove of pine bushes that was once my castle's fortress, I race up the hill to the top, where the little house that served as my castle is perched. I walk off the sandy slope of the hill onto the asphalt dead-end at the top and see my father's convertible sitting in front of the house. The engine starts up as I walk to the passenger's side door. A final glance toward the horizon impresses a sinister sight.

The pine bushes sway scarily in the wind. The ocean roars mightily and out of sight. The clouds on the horizon are shadowy and looming in the moonlight. The silhouettes of the cliffs stretch across the sand and throw everything else into a menacing darkness, a field of unknowing.

It is terrifying, but it is my kingdom…
My haven…
My home.

About the Author

Born and raised in the heart of Wine Country (a.k.a. Napa, California), Raena Fisk began writing poetry at the age of fourteen, which inspired her to eventually try her hand at short stories and essays. Along with writing, her hobbies include making frequent trips to the beach, trying new foods, cosplaying, singing, and video games. Her family and friendships are what she holds most dear, and she considers her greatest achievement to date to be her bilinguality in English and Spanish. She is currently pursuing a degree in Journalism at Fullerton College, in Fullerton, CA.

The Savior
of the World

Eli Giancanteri

"I have said these things to you, that in me you may have

peace.

In the world you will have tribulation.

But take heart; I have overcome the world."

John 16:33 (Jesus)

The story I am about to tell you is a story well known around the world, yet it is a story that is not taken to heart and believed by a lot of people in our day and age. It is the story of Jesus Christ. The Holy Bible is the book this story comes from. It was written by many different people, including Jesus' apostles and various prophets who God appointed. The story begins in a tiny, dirty manger in Bethlehem where Jesus was born.

When Jesus was born, he fulfilled an old testament prophesy. He was foretold to be born in a manger in Bethlehem, born of a virgin, and his name will be called Immanuel. This virgin the Bible speaks of is Mary. She was visited by the angel Gabriel who told her that she would give birth to a son, to name him Jesus, and that he will rule as king for all eternity and save humanity. She was perplexed at first since she was only a teenager at the time and never had any sexual relations with her husband Joseph. However, Gabriel told her that the Lord will come upon her and make this possible. So, she submitted to God's will after hearing this.

People would expect the Son of God to come down on a white, majestic horse, holding a massive sword with beams of light and rolls of thunder coming out of the sky. He is the king of the world after all. So, why did he come in the manner which he did? He came as a humble servant, as a man, born in a manger full of animals and filth. This shows he was not concerned with a glorious entrance or demanding praise from every human being of the world because of his glory. He had a much bigger plan ahead of him that God had given him: to take on every sin of man and put it on the cross with him.

The people of Bethlehem knew he was the Messiah of prophesy. Three kings from a distant land even came to bring him gifts. They were astronomers who followed the star of Bethlehem to see the birth of the king.

After his birth, Jesus grew up like any Jewish boy would. He grew up in Jerusalem. The Bible is not too detailed about his childhood other than explaining how when he was twelve, he was having deep theological and spiritual conversations with the teachers of the law in the temple. This shows even at a young age, he was divinely and spiritually gifted by his father, who is God. Then after this, the Bible goes straight into Jesus' adulthood. The first thing it records him doing is getting baptized by John the Baptist. He was baptized in the Jordan River. Although John was baptizing Jewish people for confession of sins and a chance to get right with God, we know Jesus doesn't need repentance of sins. He is God. So why did he get baptized? In his own words he said, "Let it now be so, for thus it is fitting for us to fulfill all righteousness." Even though he had no sins to repent of, it shows that the righteousness he wanted to fulfill was the righteousness not required of him, but of every sinful man.

After his baptism in the Jordan, he traveled all throughout Judea, Samaria, and Galilee, fulfilling his Father's will of seeking and saving the lost. He performed many miracles and taught numerous sermons and parables to people and gained many followers. However, he also developed many enemies, especially the Pharisees. These were the Jewish scholars and teachers in that time. They hated him because he threatened their security, prestige, and wealth in the Roman society. Anyone who took heed to Rome's political and military authority, they could go about their business and do whatever. The Pharisees wanted to keep it that way. Jesus rebuked them many times, calling them hypocrites because they taught things, yet didn't do it themselves. He also rebuked them for being too concerned about their ranking, money, and respect of the people when it is really about helping people to see the real leader and Rabbi, who is Jesus Christ.

Jesus had appointed twelve apostles or in other words, followers of him, and gave them the great commission which was to preach the gospel across the nations. This commission carries over for Christians to obey as well. Most of the apostles wrote their own books of the Bible and did many miracles and led people to Christ as well. One of the apostles Judas, betrayed Jesus for thirty pieces of silver and turned him in to the Pharisees, while Jesus was praying in the Garden of Gethsemane. The Pharisees turned him over to Pilate, who was the governor of Rome at that time and accused him of blasphemy and false accusations that he is the Messiah sent by God or "The King of the Jews." The crowd shouted to crucify him at the trial. Pilate had no choice but to follow the people's wish, even though he found no evidence to crucify him.

The very people that welcomed Jesus with much celebration and joy into Jerusalem are the same people that sent him to the cross. They turned away from their Messiah. However, Jesus knew this fate was coming. It was his whole purpose for coming into this world. He told his disciples that he would be crucified but would rise again on the third day and why that was going to take place. He knew it was the Father's will, to die for the sins of mankind. Jesus was so scared to do this he was sweating blood and asked God to allow the responsibility to pass from him. He didn't want to experience the pain and suffering. But, he knew he had too.

He wore a crown of thorns on his head, nails were pierced through his hands and feet, he was whipped, mocked and beaten, then hung on a cross to die. Jesus was innocent, and Pilate and the Pharisees knew that. Pilate was just following the will of the people, while the Pharisees wanted to keep their fame and prestige in Rome. Jesus died to forgive every single sinner of the world. The very death that we deserve, he paid the price instead, so that we can be free from our sins and live forever with Him in eternity. He even forgave the very people that put him on the cross! He said, "Father, forgive them. For they know not what they do." When Jesus died, Joseph, of Arimathea, buried him in a tomb and sealed it. But low and behold, Jesus rose again on the third day just as he foretold! He then ascended to heaven after forty days of revealing himself to everyone. Now, he sits at the right hand of the Father. This truly is the Messiah!

About the Author

Eli Giancanteri is eighteen years old and lives in Grand Terrace, California. He has a big heart for people and the Lord. He grew up in a Christian home and learned the ways of being a true Christian. As he got older, he better understood who and what Jesus is and how big of an impact He has in Eli's life. Having compassion and love for people has always been one of Eli's most important morals, and he hopes his story will spark an interest or desire to know more about God and His love for you. Eli is also a determined, goal-driven, and motivated person who strives to do his best in everything he does. He is looking forward to one day being able to express his love for people and helping others by being a firefighter.

Growing Up Too Fast

Destiny Green

"You never know how strong you are until being strong is the only option you have."

Bob Marley

"Ahhhhh." she screams as she gave birth to a baby girl. She had brown skin and bold baby blue eyes. Her name was Vanessa. Everyone in the hospital thought Vanessa was the best baby they ever laid hands on. She did not cry too much, only when she was hungry. Vanessa's mother was able to leave the hospital the very next day. June 2, 1996, Vanessa was checked out the hospital. "Off she goes home," says the nurse with the long black hair. Hearing, "Surprise," as they walked into their home. Her whole family was there waiting to meet the new baby girl. Vanessa's eyes opened wide as she looked at faces she had never seen. Months went by, and Vanessa went from a baby who did not cry to a baby who always cried. Vanessa's mother worked three jobs with very long hours, just to feed her baby girl. The late night cries and early morning stress was too much to handle. So, she decided to give Vanessa up for adoption because she could not handle the pressure of motherhood anymore. December 8, 1997, Vanessa finally got to meet her foster parents. They gave her a life her birth mother was not able to give her.

Years went by, and it was Vanessa's fifteenth birthday. She invited all of her close friends and family to celebrate her special day. Outside someone was screamed, "No, I need to see my daughter." Vanessa was confused and did not know who the crazy lady outside her house is looking for. Vanessa walked outside her house and said to the lady, "Who are you and why are you here?" The crazy lady responded, "I am your mother, and I'm here because I miss my baby girl." Vanessa gave a confused and lost look to her foster parents. The foster parents did not say a word but removed the crazy lady from outside their home. Vanessa did not believe what the crazy lady had said and enjoyed the rest of her day. The very next day, her foster parents wanted to have a talk with her. They sat down at the kitchen and began to explain what happened at Vanessa's birthday party. Vanessa stared out the kitchen window as her foster parents said, "We are not your biological parents." Tears began to roll off her chubby cheeks. She was hurt and upset because she felt as if her whole life was a lie and that she had grown up with a family that wasn't hers.

Vanessa took it upon herself to find the lady from the party again. Vanessa went to grocery stores, train stations, and hospitals trying to find her. One day, Vanessa was walking down the street, and she saw the crazy lady from the party again. But, that time she didn't look too well. Vanessa and the crazy lady sat down on a bench and talked about her past life. Vanessa began to cry as she spoke. The lady began to tell Vanessa that she was her biological mother. She froze as if her world had come to an end. She wanted answers.

After she talked with her biological mother, she went home to get answer from her foster parents. "We never wanted to hurt you. We just didn't know when the time was right to tell you about your mother," said her foster parents as Vanessa packed her clothes. "Where are you going?" asked Vanessa's parents. "I'm going to stay with my mother," said Vanessa. Her foster parents were not too happy about her decision, but they gave her a chance to make her own decision. She moved in with her biological mother, really not knowing who she was. So after she moved in, she then realized her mother used drugs.

Vanessa was only sixteen years old when she dropped out of high school and decided to take care of her biological mother. Her biological mother was diagnosed with cancer. A couple of years went by and her mother passed away. She finally got to feel part of herself. Vanessa wanted to get away from everything and everyone. So, she decided to leave the small town called Brawley. She's in the Big Apple now, New York City. She did not know anyone in the city. She was alone with no money and nowhere to go. Vanessa became homeless. One day, she was laying on the dirty ground when an older man approached her. He introduced himself as Jeff. He asked her why was she out in the streets alone. From that day, they became good friends. He helped her get an apartment on the 26th floor and a black jeep with a sun roof. She had everything she ever wanted. She soon fell in love with him.

Love turned into hate within months. He started beating her. She did not try to leave him because he would always apologize, but the apologies became frequent. He would beat her so bad that her face would begin to bleed. She had no one to turn to or anyone to talk to. She was alone. Days went by and all she could think about was if she never left her foster parents or what if she had never met her biological mother.

On August 24, 2013, Jeff got laid off at his job, and he came home furious. Vanessa was in the kitchen making dinner when he came home. He approached her and pushed her against the wall and began to say, "They fired me." Vanessa did not know what to do because she did not have a job or any money. He then proceeded to check his saving account and saw it only had $15.68. Jeff started to throw knifes, glass, and anything that was in arm's reach. "I'm sorry," said Vanessa, in a hysterical voice. He did not want an apology from her, so he beat her until she blacked out.

Hours later, she woke up on the kitchen floor in a pile of blood. She went into the restroom and cleaned herself up. After, she walked up the stairs to the bedroom looking for Jeff. She found him lying on the ground with pills scattered on the floor. She started pacing and called 911. When the ambulance arrived, they pronounced Jeff dead. Her heart was broken, but she was relieved because he could not hurt her anymore.

Days went by, and Vanessa got a job at Lowe's. She had been throwing up and feeling sick, but she did not know why. So, she went to the doctor and learned she was pregnant. She was happy and filled with joy to be having a baby. On September 1, 2016, Vanessa has now worked at Lowe's for three years and has a beautiful young son.

About the Author

Destiny Monae Green was born on December 22, 1997. She was born and raised in a small town called Brawley, CA. She is a young, gifted African American woman with many hopes dreams. She is currently attending College of the Desert, to achieve her Associates Degree in Early Childhood Education. After she receives her AA in Early Childhood Education, she plans to move out of state to continue school at a university.

Real Life Hero

Erika Gudino

Until you have lost a very dear pet
It's hard to feel the grief one begets.
But I know the sadness you are going trough
For I have worn those very same shoes.
You look around and see a big hole;
Your home empty, your heart not whole.
But day by day may the fading tears
Bring smiling memories year after year.

John and Jenny were just beginning their life together. They were young and in love, with a perfect little house and not a care in the world. They decided to start a new life and moved to West Palm Beach, Florida to initiate the project of building their family. John was a little nervous because his wife Jenny was anxious to have a baby, and he was not sure about parenting.

One night, John surprised his wife with a lovely large orchid flower with purple and cream leaves. Jenny was so happy; she thanked John by throwing her arms around his neck and kissing him.

"Be careful not to overwater it," John warned.

After a couple days, John asked Jenny about the plant and she replied, "It died. I think I put a lot of water in it." Then, she got the real issue: "If I can't even keep a plant alive, how am I ever going to keep a baby alive?" She looked like she might start crying. John thought maybe a dog would be good practice and started looking in newspapers.

The next day, John brought home a wiggly yellow fur ball of a puppy. It was a gold Labrador retriever; Jenny could not believe she had a little baby. They decided to name the puppy "Polo." After several months, Polo quickly grew into a barreling, ninety-seven-pound brute of a Labrador retriever, a dog like no other. It was a little hard for John and Jenny that Polo was a hurricane. Polo was not obedient. If he were alone at home, he would destroy everything around. Also, there were many visits to the veterinarian and many pills to calm him down. The dog was becoming a problem. John thought it would be a good idea to enroll Polo in a school of obedience for dogs, but that was not a good idea because Polo failed every class. And yet, Polo's heart was pure. Just as he joyfully refused any limits on his behavior, his love and loyalty were boundless. Over time, John and Jenny learned to live with the antics of Polo and giving him unconditional love.

Polo was their first baby and one of the most important things in their life. When Jenny discovered she was pregnant and gave the news to John, they could not believe they would be parents. With the arrival of the baby, Polo was very excited and did not want to separate from him.

One day, John decided to barbecue at their backyard, while the baby and Polo were sleeping in the bedroom. Jenny was outside helping John get everything ready when they heard the baby crying. They both tried to run inside to get to their baby, but they couldn't open the door. They realized the house was on fire. John called 911 for help, and Jenny was desperately trying to get inside, but the smoke was too heavy, and the door started falling. Jenny was crying uncontrollably and had lost all hope of seeing her child again.

Finally, the firefighters arrived on the scene. The house had heavy fire burning from both the first and second floors. They could hear the baby crying and acted quickly. It was not easy to get to the second floor where Polo and the baby were. After a long time of struggle, the firefighters got into the house and started looking for the baby. When they finally got to the bedroom, they could not believe what they saw. The baby was kept relatively safe by Polo, as he used his body to shield the infant from the flames. In turn, he only suffered burns on his arm and side. Polo and the baby were taken to the hospital immediately as well as John and Jenny because they had suffered minor burns on their hands and face when trying to enter the house to save their baby.

After reviewing the baby, the doctor said he would recover, but he must be in the hospital for a couple of weeks. John and Jenny were so grateful to Polo that he had saved the life of her baby, but they were very worried about whether or not know if Polo would recover.

After a week, the baby was ready to come home. But Polo was still severe, as he had inhaled all the smoke and had been close to the flames that had burned his body and destroyed his lungs. The vet told John that Polo was suffering a lot and would not be a normal dog anymore. He would require much care, and it would be very costly. John was devastated and did not know what to do. John could let Polo recovered slowly, but he would not be the same and would also have pain for the rest of his life, or he could let Polo go, so he could rest in peace. It was very difficult for John and Jenny to make the decision. Polo was part of their lives. They had loved him since he was a puppy, and they didn't want to lose him.

With all the pain in his heart, John decided to let Polo go. That day, John and Jenny were in the room with Polo. They could not hold back the tears and the pain they felt. With tears in his eyes, John said to Polo: "I hope you know how much I loved you all of your life. You were always there when I needed you. Through life or death, I will always love you." After his words, Polo moved his tail, and he closed his eyes. Polo was gone. John and Jenny were very sad, but at the same time, they knew their friend was resting in peace, and he would be always in their hearts forever. **He showed them** what love can do. Polo had given his life for the baby who meant everything to John and Jenny. Polo became a hero and a symbol of true love.

About the Author

Erika Gudino a twenty-one year old college student living in Palm Desert, California. She is native of Barstow, California and was raised in Mexicali, BC Mexico. While she lived in Mexicali, she graduated from high school. She went to a beauty school for six months and earned her certificate as a nail technician and started her first job in a beauty salon. Erika had a passion for animals and always wanted to learn new things. Also, she became a certified dog groomer. When she became an adult, she went back to California and started college. She is studying to be a registered nurse while raising her two-year-old child.

Operation Wildflower Rescue

Rhonda Hakim

My mother taught me to feel, to love,
My mother taught me to cry, to laugh.
My mother taught me goodness and beauty,
But fate snatched her away suddenly.
Since she was taken I have no rest.
She was my life's vivifying breath.

"LAST NIGHT"

Last night you were here, you came home to me.
You caressed me, loved me, like in the old days.
It couldn't have been a dream, it felt like reality,
I could hear your voice, see your dear face.
The two of us talked and you told me everything,
How you thought about us there, how you were worrying.

"I ALWAYS KNEW"

I always knew how much I loved you,
That I could never leave you behind.
My body may be a worthless worm,
But my soul from yours will never be torn.
Years were passing and the horrible curse came true.
They locked us millions in cattle cars,
And even to you, so faithful to the Almighty,
The murderers denied immunity.
I couldn't do for you a thing.
Watching you my eyes were weeping.
I wanted to follow you everywhere – even
At the price of my life, I thought then.
But on a horrible night, as our train
Slowed down and stopped in the open plain,
They stole you from me, my only treasure.
And yet, I could continue on further.
When the snow fell, I worried about you only,
You were by my side at every step.
When I got tired, you led me ahead,
You stroked me, you held my hand.
This is how I survived the dreadfully big struggle
And I returned to the old abode.
Since then I always search to find you, to reunite,
I expect you morning, noon, and night.
I always knew how much I loved you.
My soul has never left you, followed you even then.
And down here, lifelessly, I play a farce – I mime,
This world is no longer mine.
by Magdalena Klein

Holly Plants a Seed

When I met Scarlet Gilia, she was not someone who particularly mattered in my world. Scarlet was a citizen of the underworld, a prostitute high on anything but life. Her existence was tumultuous and untamed, and as a civilized woman, it never occurred to me that I should ever attempt to befriend someone like Scarlet. It's not that I was too good or that I didn't care. After all, I am a counselor at Caladium Community College. I have built my career on cultivating the dreams and paths of young minds. It just never occurred to me that I could or should impact the life of this misguided wildflower. Then, one Friday afternoon, as I headed towards home, my eyes winced past the glare of the sun and caught a glimpse of tears stained on the face of a seemingly destitute young woman there on a bus bench.

I thought to mind my own business, but my heart was set on guilting my head, and before I knew it, I had parked my car at the nearby café, and I was walking towards this woman who was sitting at the bus bench. I stood behind in her shadow for a moment observing her presence. Her long brown hair was tussled and dirty, her eyes dulled with hopelessness. She was almost childlike and something inside me said, "This is someone's daughter." I quickly sat down on the bench with plans to say something that would matter. Scarlet sniffled with remarkable determination to compose herself and hide a visibly busted lip.

Our eyes met briefly, as I fumbled for words, "Are you okay? What's your name?" I didn't know what else to ask in that awkward moment.

She ignored me, but after some coaxing, she finally snarled back, "My name is Scarlet if you must know, and yes, I'm perfectly fine, and I really didn't ask you to barge into my business." I gasped in offense and stood up to walk away, but my heart was still in "do-good' mode. Before I knew it, I had invited her to join me for lunch at the Foxglove Café across the street.

At first, our words were few, as we looked over the lunch menu. Once we had placed our order, a bit of small talk ensued.

"Scarlet's a nice name. Is that your real name?" I said.

"Does it matter?" retorted Scarlet. Honestly, at that point, it really didn't matter. We were strangers, and I was imposing myself into her world. I just couldn't help wondering how a young woman like Scarlet made the decision to become a prostitute. I'm certain it was not a lifelong dream, and it couldn't possibly be fulfilling. So why? *How did she come to this place,* I wondered? I began asking her about the circumstances that drove her to these choices.

I asked her if she had family and where she had grown up. As it turned out, she had grown up in a very supportive home but had experienced abuse at the hands of a family friend. Believing it was her fault, she remained silent for a few years while the abuse continued. One day, at the age of eleven, when anger and bravery welled up in her chest, she went to her mother and spoke about the abuse. Thankfully, the abuse was immediately put to an end, but the memories continued to churn with perpetual torment.

I too had been through a similar abuse when I was young. My world could have ended up much like that of Scarlet's if it were not for Janie Marigold, a woman in our neighborhood, who had befriended me when I was a young teenager. She had a similar experience in her childhood, and she was the one person that I could always talk to. In many ways, Janie mentored and taught me how to be the strong woman I am today. As I grew up, I knew I wanted to make a difference in the lives of young people as they made critical decisions about how to obtain their dreams. I wanted to be a real and present force that could help another human being find their calling.

As I looked at the young, broken woman sitting across from me, I imagined her future as bright, so I began speaking life into her world. I also told her about my own experience and how I had long blamed myself for what happened even when others told me I hadn't done anything wrong. I told her it took some time for me to get to a place where I could walk away from the hurt to become the woman I am today.

In my own days at college, I had conducted research for one of my psychology classes that encompassed statistics and facts about teenagers and adults of childhood abuse. I knew from research that many victims, like Scarlet and me, become hostage to the memories. As a result, many young victims of abuse never step into their destined calling. Instead, they seek out perpetual abuse, believing it be their sole worth. Scarlet was indeed a textbook case in her own right. I could only hope that our brief encounter might be the spark that called her out into the light.

Halfway through lunch, a largely-built, angry man tattered with misogynist tattoos, came bursting through the café doors. His words spewed venom at Scarlet, who cowered and began apologizing. I stood up and positioned myself between them. I tried to convince her that she did not have to apologize to him. As I was speaking to her, the brut took hold of my shoulders and shoved me out of the way, telling me to mind my own business, as he yanked her up by the arm.

"Scarlet! Scarlet!" I cried. "Don't go with him. Come with me. You can come with me." I was frantic and felt helpless to save her. One moment, we were enjoying lunch over a bit of chit chat, and the next moment, she was angrily screaming at me in the middle of the café.

"You don't know my life. You don't know me. You think you can save the world 'miss do-gooder?' Well, you can't. This is my world. This is who I am. Sorry to disappoint you, but you can't really save everyone." I was dumbfounded and silenced with mortal shock at the turn of events, fashioned with that proverbial jaw to the floor look. I sheepishly gathered myself together, paid the bill, and headed for my car.

As I walked through the parking lot, I scanned the streets looking for Scarlet and the thug that had heartlessly whisked her away. My chest was pounding as I got into my car and slumped down into the driver's seat. I shouted and sobbed, pounding my fist to the steering wheel until frustration wore itself out. I then composed myself, tidying up my face, combing my hands through my hair to look as if nothing happened. My hands clumsily put the key into the ignition, and I drove home. Once I had settled in for the night, thoughts filled my head about the young woman Scarlet and about the many victims who succumb to hopelessness.

Over the next few days, Scarlet stayed in my thoughts. I couldn't get her out of my head, so I decided to pay a visit to my dear friend Janie. She was getting older in years but still as beautiful as ever. We talked over a cup of tea about days gone by. I told her how her friendship with me had made a difference in my life, and then, I told her about Scarlet. Janie said she once had been befriended by a woman who also mentored her. Talking to Janie always made things better. I told her if I ran into Scarlet again, I too would offer to mentor her if she would let me. At the end of the evening, Janie and I hugged, and upon leaving, I promised to visit her more often.

Over the days and weeks that flew by, I drove down the street, sat at the bus bench, ate lunch in the Foxglove Café but never caught a glimpse of Scarlet. I kept trying to find her everywhere I went. I prayed for her safety and wondered what had become of her. I held onto the hope that possibly words I had spoken into her life had resonated with her soul, that maybe she finally decided to give life a fighting chance. With no concrete answers, I moved on from that experience, but I took to heart that chance meeting. Every time, I counseled a new college student, I thought of Scarlet and longed for her to walk through those doors. If only she had a reason to dream.

Scarlet's New Beginnings

I'm Scarlet Gilia, but you can call me Scarlet. Holly is the woman who befriended me at the bus bench. When I met Holly, she seemed like a nice woman, but she was one of those "do-good" people. She meant well, but I was sure she was wasting her time. I was a prostitute, and she was clearly a successful woman who had her life all figured out. As far as I was concerned, we had nothing in common. My head just wasn't in the right place. I had never really believed in myself.

Truth be told, I never imagined a future beyond those mean streets. When I was thirteen, I began drinking and getting high on street drugs. I had been abused for a time, and the street drugs had a way of dulling the memories. My parents tried to help, but I was determined to self-destruct. One day, I ran away and found myself living at a party house. Eventually, a fellow partier introduced me to a pimp. When Holly and I met, I had already been in the game for about seven years. I wasn't ready to walk away though I appreciated the sentiments.

I was awful sorry about the way I blew up at her. She was awful nice; I must have seemed terribly ungrateful. It's just that when my pimp showed up, things got a little crazy. I didn't want anyone to get hurt, and I didn't want more trouble than I was already in. After I left, I thought about Holly often. She had mentioned she had gone through abuse as well. I wondered how life would have turned out differently if I could have just let go of the past. Maybe, I could have been a career woman or at least lived a nicer life. It's just that, my road had long been paved and looking back this all seemed impossible at the time.

When I ran into Janie, I was running for my life. The pimp had left me at a motel and had come back drunk and abusive as usual. Only that time, it seemed worse. Either that or Holly's words had gotten to me. I just knew I needed to get away quickly; that's when I bolted from the room. I found myself in a nearby shopping center, looking for unlocked cars to hide in.

Janie called out to me, "Excuse me, miss, but are you in some sort of trouble?"

I frantically begged her to hide me. Before I knew it, I was in her car, and we were speeding away from the area. She drove for miles before stopping at a donut shop where we sat and spoke for quite some time. Again, there I was sitting across from another woman who wasted no time in trying to save me from myself. We shared stories of childhood experiences, and I found myself defending my path to a woman who once again had been through a similar childhood but had successfully made her way in life. That time, something in me chose to listen. We had long been chatting when Janie mentioned she never got my name.

"It's Scarlet. My name is Scarlet," I said. I'll never forget that look on her face.

She said, "Scarlet? You're Scarlet, as in Scarlet Gilia?" We laughed a bit, and then, she told me about her friendship with Holly. It was then that I realized that life was about to change for the better. In an unexpected turn, Janie offered to take me in for a brief time to help me get on my feet. I accepted her offer and went home with her that evening. I don't know how she did it, but over the course of a few days, Janie inspired me to make a new life for myself. I agreed to enter a drug rehabilitation facility. Later, I worked towards my GED, and one day, I paid a visit to Janie to thank her for all she had done for me. We talked about the possibility of college, and once again, Janie spoke real dreams into my life.

Janie Marigold Blooms a Mission

I'm Janie, the woman you've heard about throughout this story. When I met Scarlet, she was on the brink of saving herself. It was really all her. At that time, I didn't know how things would turn out, but it was clear to me that Scarlet had a calling that somehow involved me and Holly. As if her calling might also be our calling. I suspected that once Scarlet had cleaned up, she would come back into our lives with a clear head and a fistful of dreams. In hindsight, I probably should have called Holly to tell her who I had run into, but I felt that to help Scarlet, we needed to first let her fly. She needed to find her own strength, and indeed, she did just that.

When she came back, there was a new spark in her eyes. Scarlet was a woman ready to take on the world. I talked to her about going to college and mentioned that Holly was a counselor at Caladium Community College. Scarlet seemed eager to meet Holly again. I called up Holly and invited her to dinner. I mentioned I had invited a lovely young lady to dinner who could use some college advice. Holly agreed to join us that evening, so I busied myself with dinner plans and asked Scarlet to set the table.

When Holly arrived, Scarlet answered the door and said, "Hello, Holly. How are you?"

Holly took a second look and then said, "Scarlet? Is that you, Scarlet? What on earth are you doing here?"

After things settled down, I said to the ladies, "Come, sit down, and let's talk about all of this over dinner." The evening carried on with tears and laughter. Holly and Scarlet both agreed that a psychology degree would be a great path for Scarlet. I said, "You know, it's something the way the three of us have come together."

We realized that evening that the key to each of our paths was the person who inspired us to heal and grow, and together, we decided to create a network of mentors who could reach out to young abuse survivors who just needed someone who understood. Like the old saying goes, "It takes a village." I'd like to think that it takes a few wildflowers to inspire one small seed to bloom into its calling.

About the Author

Rhonda Hakim grew up in Orange County, California. She is a writer, marketing professional, and computer geek, who is working towards starting a non-profit organization called *Operation Wildflower Rescue* with the goal of mentoring victims of child abuse. As an abuse survivor, Rhonda is eager to be at the forefront of making a difference in the lives of many survivors. In her free time, she enjoys roller skating and hiking the many trails in her town.

Reunited

Urooj Khan

"Nothing is permanent in this wicked world,
not even our troubles."

Charlie Chaplin

The dark-haired girl was fast walking away from the group that was touring the town, picking up their phones or wallets from their pockets as she went by. He noticed her from afar; he was not much of a person to go and confront, but just observe. Eric decided to go back home. He turned on the silver Mercedes Benz he was in and drove off. The girl, Jackie, was not so unaware of the silver Mercedes she had seen around. She hoped it was not an undercover cop. Jackie wanted to figure out why the car was following her, but at that moment, she wanted to see how much she made. She went into the narrow alley, counted the money from the wallets, and went to get lunch before it was dark. Not knowing when she could see the silver Mercedes again, she started planning what to say and how to react if it were an undercover police officer.

Eric knew she was smart, but he did not realize she knew he was following her around. He still did not know how to tell her what he knew about her. He looked in the full-size mirror at his reflection. While the sun was setting, he was thinking of how he could approach her. Jackie knew of a cozy place to sleep, but she had to get there before any other person could take her spot. She was glad she could rest on a full stomach. The city was getting dark; the shadows were all displayed on the tall buildings. She appreciated the view she had the pleasure of seeing, as she went on her way.

After getting to the place that she had slept in for many nights, she lay down on her back and thought about her life – how she got to where she was and what the future would hold. All she remembered was being in a hospital-like place for kids. She never got along with other kids and did not want to either. Then, she went with a friendly couple to their house for some time. After that, she was with a single mom in an apartment, but she always returned to that institution for kids. It was nice and colorful, but it did not feel nice to stay there. When she was old enough to leave, she had nowhere to go, so she made herself a bed out of objects she found in neighborhoods of wealthy people and started pickpocketing as a means to get food and water. Jackie questioned if life would be different for her or if that was all she would do.

One day, instead of going to college, Eric was at home in his lavish room doing his homework. The sun was shining brightly facing his room. While he was working on his laptop, it seemed to be really hot, so he went to open one of the large windows. He opened it and before turning back to continue his work, he saw Jackie. Eric did not know who she was, but she looked familiar. By the time he went down the spiral staircase and out of the enormous house, she was out of sight.

The next time he saw her was in the market place. He was passing by when he happened to look her way. She was sitting on a curb looking at the people around her. Eric watched as she got up, passed by a business man having his coffee, but after passing by him, she had a thick, leather men's wallet in her hands. He realized she had found what she was looking for. He understood that she might be in a bad situation and decided to go on as if he did not know or see anything. After thinking about the matter over numerous times, he wanted to meet with her and talk, but to that day, he still had not been able to do that. Weeks of following her around made him feel uneasy, but he had to know about her.

It was a warm, busy Saturday in the already crowded market. Jackie knew that was the perfect time to score. Eric felt Jackie knew that and went to the market. By the time Eric got there, Jackie had already gotten a watch from a snooty-looking man, while he was arguing with an elderly shopkeeper. Jackie saw the silver Mercedes show up. She hid to see if the person would come out, as she never got to see this person's face, as the windows were tinted. A familiar looking man with dark brown hair and round trendy sunglasses, that covered his eyes, got out of the car. He took them off and was looking around the market. Jackie thought he was dressed extremely dressy and too rich to be a policeman. She came out from her hiding place and walked confidently with long strides to the man to find out why he had been following her for the past month.

Eric decided he was tired of hiding and wanted to talk to her that day. As he got out of the car, she disappeared. He was puzzled as to where she went as he had just seen her. He did not have to be confused for long, as she appeared out of nowhere right in front of him. She saw that his eyes were dark brown exactly like hers, and they just stared at each other. When she was closer to him, she realized he did look familiar, really familiar, but she could not figure out how she knew him. She was baffled as to how she would know the person driving the expensive car, wearing designer sunglasses and clothes. Eric had never seen her up close, and he finally believed the files he had found.

"You're my sister," said Eric, as he handed her the file. Jackie was stunned as she took the manila folder and opened it. Eric and Jackie were both from the same orphanage and had come from the same home originally because they were siblings. Eric was adopted by a wealthy family, and Jackie was left to fend for herself. She realized why he looked familiar. He was all that she had when her parents passed away, but she was too young to remember any of it.

About the Author

Urooj Khan is sixteen years old. She is the youngest of five siblings. Her parents are from Mumbai, India. This is her first year at Fullerton College. She is majoring in Biology. She is planning to transfer to a four-year university here in California. She has always enjoyed reading, swimming, and spending time with her friends and family, and now, she is interested in writing as well.

How I Got a Cat

Alicia Loredo

"Good things can come from unexpected places."

Last Man

It was the last week of high school. My mom and her boyfriend were out of town on a trip to Mexico, which left my brother and me with the house all to ourselves. One day, I came home to find my bother in our backyard staring at the fence. I went outside, and I asked him what he was staring at, to which he replied with an abrupt "Shh!" I was confused at first, but once I got closer to the fence, I began to hear tiny meows. After identifying the sound, I began to look for the source of the tiny meows. That is when my brother pointed to a gap between the fence that separated our house from the alley and one that kept trees from growing on our lawn. Hidden in that spot, there were about five of the cutest kittens I had ever seen. Three of the kittens were all black, and the rest were white. All of them had bright baby blue eyes.

I looked to my brother and asked him, "What should we do?" He shrugged his shoulders and went inside the house. My brother and I knew better than to remove the kittens from the fence. If we did, then our scent would be all over those kittens, and the mother would not want to take care of them. I then followed my brother back into the house. A few hours passed by, and I decided to go outside and check on the fence kittens. All of them are gone except one small black cat. I looked all around the backyard, but none of the other kittens were to be found. It looked as if the little black cat that was left behind was the runt of the litter, and the mother had left it behind.

In nature, mothers will often do this to their young if they believe that they will not survive in the wild. I went inside and grabbed a shoe box and a rag. After, I went back outside to where the small kitten was. Using the rag, I attempted to grab the kitten and put it inside the shoe box. It was not an easy task at first because the kitten was so frightened at the sight of me.

Once I finally got the kitten in the box, I took it inside. Unsure of what to do next, I proceeded to google everything I needed to know about caring for a young kitten. My brother and I were prepared to care for that kitten until it was big enough to give away. We gathered all the necessary supplies needed for the little kitten after a quick stop at PetSmart.

I knew once my mom came home from her vacation, the kitten would have to leave. My mother, brother, and I had allergies when it came to cats. My mother's allergies were more severe than the rest of ours. For the next few days, my brother and I would take turns caring for the kitten. We kept the kitten in the shoe box, in the corner of our living room, on the couch. While I was finishing school, my bother would watch the cat, and once I got home, I would watch the cat. The kitten was too young to eat dry or wet food, so we had feed it with a bottle. There was a special formula that is used when feeding young cats, similar to baby formula. Taking care of the kitten was not a challenge. At that age the kitten wasn't very active. The majority of the time, the kitten would be eating and sleeping.

The week went by fast, and it was Friday. I was done with school until the graduation ceremony, and my mom was expected to come home that night. My mom came home around 10pm. We were happy to see she made it home safe. She began to talk about all the things she did on her trip to Mexico. It was not long before she noticed a mysterious shoe box in our living room. She approached the box and opened it. She was surprised to see a little black fuzzy kitten sleeping in the box. I explained what had happened to the kitten, and to my surprise, she understood and let us continue taking care of the kitten. She let me care for it until we found a good home for the little cat. Despite being allergic to cats, my mom enjoyed having the cat around the house. She enjoyed bottle feeding the cat most of all. With time, we figured out if I bathed the kitten often, we are all less likely to have allergies.

Tuesday was the day of my graduation ceremony. I graduated from Fullerton Union High School. It was a big and nice ceremony. A lot of friends and family showed up to it. After the ceremony, everyone came over to our house for dinner. It was a great dinner; everyone was enjoying themselves. Everyone also admired the kitten that was temporarily staying at our house. One of my cousins then asked me if I was going to keep the kitten. I found it an appropriate time to ask my mom if she would let me keep the cat instead of giving it away. Surprisingly, her reply was yes. She said I could keep the kitten only if I take care of it and bathe it regularly. Without hesitation, I agreed to my mom's conditions.

The following Saturday, we took the cat to the family vet to get all of its necessary shots and vaccinations. That is when we found out the gender of the cat was male. It was more difficult than I expected to determine the gender of cats while they are young. I decided to name him Julian, after the lead singer in my favorite band. After Julian's vaccinations, we bought him a blue collar with a name tag. We also got him cat toys and a cat tree. Lastly, we got him a litter box and a large black cat bed to officially welcome him into his new permanent home. My mom and my brother enjoy having Julian around. We are all glad to have him as part of our home.

About the Author

Alicia Loredo graduated from Fullerton Union High school, in July 2016. She has always been fond of animals since she was a little girl. She currently owns two cats, two dogs, and three birds. While Alicia is not taking care of her animals, she likes to spend her time painting or playing piano. In the future, she hopes to find happiness and serenity wherever life takes her.

The Footsteps

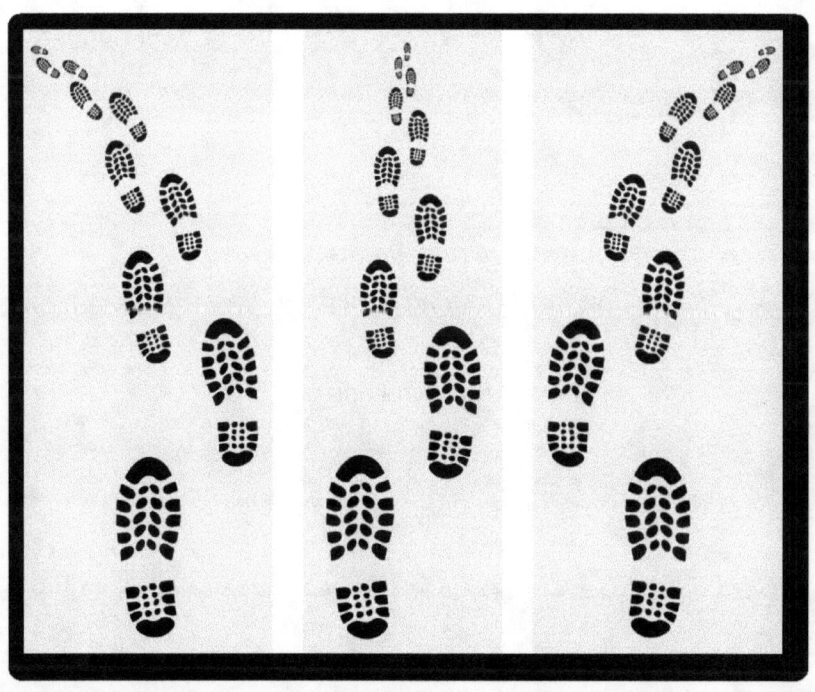

Alma Munguia

"Monsters are real, ghosts are real too.
They live inside us, and sometimes, they win."

Stephen King

I still remember the first time I heard the footsteps. I remember it like it was yesterday. It was a warm, October evening. The leaves were turning; homes were decorated with spider webs, ghouls and pumpkins. I was walking home through the entrails of the city. It had been a long hectic day at work. I left work that night hungry and exhausted. Normally, I would take the long way home, the scenic route. I sure did love that route. I would wander on the nice side of town, pass all of our historical landmarks, the creek and the fields. Tonight, I was too exhausted to take that route. I just wanted to be home. So, I took the short way.

I was cutting through one of the sketchy alleyways near my job when I first heard them. The alleys weren't a nice place for a young girl to go through at night. There were all sorts of low-life people in this area. The downtown area was known to hold its fair share of gang members and violent junkies. So, you can imagine how terrified I was when I heard the footsteps.

I was walking through an alley, nearly halfway to the end when I began to hear someone walking behind me. I was immediately filled with terror. I remember my mind construing the worst scenarios possible. I had no doubt in my mind that at any given moment something bad was going to occur. I began to pick up my pace. I was walking faster and faster. Yet the footsteps were picking up. They were following me. Whoever was following me was sure to get me.

My heart was beating out of my chest. My breathing had become rapid and shallow. I was horrified. I began to take off as rapidly as my body allowed me. I was ready to run a quick turn to the right at the end of the alleyway. When I was about to reach the corner, I turned my head back and looked at what was behind me. To my amazement, there was no one. Not a single soul was in that alleyway. I sprinted all the way home, thanking God for saving me and sending whoever my harasser was on a different route. It wasn't until weeks later that I discovered what was following me home that day wasn't human, and it wasn't the end.

The footsteps would appear at odd times throughout the day. At first it took me three weeks to hear the footsteps again after my first encounter. Then, I began to hear them more often until it was multiple times a day. I recall one day where I heard them as I was speaking to my mother. We were conversing about visiting my grandmother in Denver when I heard them creeping behind me. I attempted to disregard them as calmly as I could, but I couldn't fool Mother. That night, I overheard my parents talking about my sudden personality change. They were planning to send me to a therapist. I didn't blame them.

At that point I had heard the steps 27 times, 27 horrifying times. You would expect for each time to get less and less frightful, but it didn't. It grew eerier each time. Each time, it got longer. Each time it gets closer. They were haunting me, taunting me. It began to make me feel as if though I were going insane. I was petrified. Sometimes I'd run for miles. Some days, I'd run until my lungs felt as if though they're going to collapse inside my body. In the beginning, I would hear the footsteps sparingly, but as time went on, they began to terrorize me more until they were an almost normal part of my life.

I was afraid as I would turn every corner. I was terror-stricken when I would turn my lights off at night to go to sleep. I was anxious when I would go into the bathroom to shower. I would tremble when I was alone. I never knew when they'd be back. It could be back at any given moment. I was terrified, and I couldn't live my life like that anymore. I wasn't sure how much longer I could handle it. I was bound to explode at any moment. It had to come to an end. I didn't know what to do anymore.

I could hardly eat. I could hardly sleep. I couldn't carry on normal social interactions with anyone anymore. The footsteps filled my mind. I couldn't think of anything else. It had to stop. If the footsteps didn't kill me themselves, they'd be the death of me. I needed help, but no one would believe me. No one would understand. Everyone already thought I was going crazy. They'd never experienced anything like that. I needed help, but from whom? Who would believe me? Who would even know what to do?

I decided to saunter over to the local chapel after school one day to obtain holy water. The chapel contains beautiful rose-stained glass windows, Victorian architecture, and dark maple pews. Although it's quaint, it's beauty is timeless. It looked like one of those chapels that you would see in old black and white movies. It had a pointed roof and a small tower with a crucifix perched gracefully on top of it. I went into the chapel and headed to the altar where the crimson white holy water fountain lay. I had seen enough horror films to know that evil spirits despise holy water. Surely, blessing myself and my room would help keep the spirit away from me for a while.

I knelt there carefully gathering some of the holy water into my bottle. I wouldn't consider myself a very religious person. As a matter of fact, that was the first time I'd stepped into a church in years. I know that the only thing that could save me from this negativity is God. I had faith in myself and in the higher power to get me through this. The spirit could only drag me down if I let it. For the first time in a long time, I felt safe inside the church.

I left the chapel, ready to head home with newfound hope. It was breezy outside that day. The trees no longer had any leaves on them. I remember the sun lightly warming my body as I walked down the street. Tranquility enveloped me, and I was content. After walking for a few moments, I began to hear footsteps behind me. I tried to brush it off, convincing myself that it was just another person trying to get to a destination like myself. For once, I was not absolutely horrified by the sound of footsteps. I continued strolling home, but after five minutes, the footsteps were still in the background. I was overridden with the sudden feeling that it surely must be them again. I continued to try to walk at my normal pace, reminding myself that no matter how fast I moved, they still always keep up with me.

My actions and image as of late, since the footsteps had appeared, had been making me act and appear aloof. I decided I didn't want to draw any more attention to myself. It was broad daylight, and the last thing I needed was the town folk seeing me run away from an invisible monster. Scared, I continued to walk casually, but then for the first time the footsteps began gaining speed on their own. I was not moving any quicker, but it seemed as if though that time they weren't just trying to scare me. They wanted to get me.

I began picking up my pace. Yet, they were walking faster and faster yet again. I began to jog lightly. I could hear them scurrying rapidly on my heels as I burst into a full sprint. They were directly behind me at that point. I must have been in fingers reach of my attacker. Out of breath and trembling in terror, I sprinted directly into my home. I ran towards the kitchen, hoping my mom would be in there fixing dinner. Surely, the footsteps would leave me alone if my mom or someone else was in my home. I got to the kitchen, but tragically, I found no one in there. The house was silent.

The footsteps had stopped running and were now approaching me, strutting slowly behind me. I ran to the end of the room and got against the wall. I was so close to the taupe kitchen wall that I was nearly hugging it. Tears were now streaming down my scorching hot face. My body was shaking. I was horrified, racking my brain thinking about what was bound to happen at any given moment. Terrified and with the last ounce of my bravery, I turned around slowly. For the first time, I saw who had been haunting me. She had pale alabaster skin, hazel green eyes, long messy dark brown hair. Her face was beautiful, serene, yet somehow twisted in a very sinister way. Her lips were curled slightly on one end. She began to open her mouth as if though she was about to say something, but her vocal chords emitted no noise.

To my shock the person standing before me was no one other than myself. My body was now becoming numbingly cold as sweat rushed down my face. My head spun like an overactive merry-go-round, and everything began to fade into a dark abyss. My knees began to give out slowly underneath me. I no longer had the strength to keep myself standing. My breathing became stagnant and weak as my decrepit body plummeted to the ground. I had gone mad.

About the Author

Alma Munguia is an up and coming author from the Los Angeles area, taking up creative writing on her free time. Alma enjoys reading various styles of literature. She takes pleasure in writing in her spare time, whether it's jotting down ideologies, poems, or even creating future excerpts for novels. When she's not creatively writing, she is producing special effects horror makeup. Her writing style has been influenced vastly by horror and the psychological mind. She hopes to write novels in the horror and thriller genres in the very near future.

DUST

Elizabeth Ojeda

Listen to the MUSTN'TS, child,

Listen to the DON'TS

Listen to the SHOULDN'TS

The IMPOSSIBLES, the WON'TS

Listen to the NEVER HAVES

Then listen close to me—

Anything can happen, child,

ANYTHING can be.

~Shel Silverstein

"Sam! Are you even listening?"

"What?"

"Oh, my god! See, this is why I don't call you."

I looked down at my smudged laptop screen, which was flooded with all of the standard windows—a blank Microsoft Word document, Google Chrome flooded with countless tabs, Spotify, providing white noise—all used to fool oneself into thinking he/she if being productive. There was a small crack at the bottom right corner, just where the clock was, so I was never really able to check the time, but I was assuming I had been skyping Alyssa for a couple of hours by then. I watched as my freckle-faced best friend continued to ramble on about her endless amount of responsibilities, which she had yet to accomplish, as she stuffed her face with a BLT Subway sandwich that she complained about almost immediately because she hated the BLT. So, why did she choose the BLT? I have no idea.

I've known Alyssa since the third grade. It's kind of a funny story actually. Alyssa hated me at first because I stole her best friend. Soon after though, her ex-best friend replaced me too, so I guess one could say we bonded over being rejects. Our friendship, just like most friendships, is built on irrationally hating the same people for their annoying ideocracies, trash talking chick flicks when they were secretly our guilty pleasure, self-depreciating humor... Must I say anymore? As much as we may seem emotionally constipated, we really do love each other. Well, at least I do, for she's the one person who has tolerated me all these years.

"You know you love me."

"Shut up." *She'll give in.*

"I love you too, bitch." *Told you so.*

Before Alyssa could restart her rant, I cut her off. "Are you going home this weekend?" Alyssa and I went to different universities, which made it hard to stay in touch sometimes. That's one of the parts of adulting that no one really mentions. She shrugged and mumbled something, but I was too distracted watching the bacon and tomato dance around in her mouth.

"Dude. Chew your damn food!"

"Alright, alright. Chill. Are you going to tell your parents this weekend?"

The silence was loud. Our childish banter came to an end. Damn it! I knew she would bring that up. My chest tightened, making it hard to breathe normally, I felt the warmth of anxiety spread to my neck and ears; my body became more sensitive to the air around me as a chill tiptoed up my spine. I knew if I told her an excuse, she wouldn't leave me alone, so I did what I do best. Lie. "Of course. I went to therapy this morning. Susan and I role played to prepare me for the ultimate showdown."

My first therapy session was pretty standard. "Tell me about yourself." I hate that question. I don't know ask my mom—actually, don't. I'm just like you. I'm a normal 20-year-old girl enrolled into a university with big hopes and dreams. I'm fairly optimistic, and just like every other naïve young adult, I feel like my purpose is to change the world for the better. I have two middle-class, loving, and supportive parents, who are happily married and constantly encouraging and reminding me that I can accomplish anything. I have a ten-year-old sister who is basically my best friend even though she gets under my skin from time to time. I live on the outskirts of Chicago, Illinois where you can find Al Capone eating a deep-dish pizza at Giordano's as sweet Jazz echoes through the streets—but, that's after you ignore the flooding in the streets, sweltering summers, subzero winters, nonexistent springs and autumns, the sound of the metal-rotating blades of the ghetto birds flying around at night in an attempt to reduce the crime in the alleyways—yeah, I love Chicago. I honestly have nothing to complain about. No broken family or financial struggles. So, why was I there?

Back in the day, I found myself either in extreme ecstasy or in suffocating desolation. During my highs, I could take on the world. You know how parents ask their kids, "If your friend jumps off a cliff, would you?" I was that friend your parents were warning you about. It was like a constant adrenaline rush, as if I had just jumped out of a plane into ice cold water with sharks swimming around me with "You Make My Dreams" by Daryl Hall & John Oates playing in the background. Dangerous, I know. Although I had more motivation to accomplish mundane tasks, like homework or even cleaning my room, with that motivation came the will to do *anything*.

I couldn't sit still. I found myself going out every other day, drinking more than I could handle, sleeping around with half the population, staying up nights at a time for no reason whatsoever. There was no control, the definition of chaos. Now, as for the lows, it was the polar opposite. Suddenly, the ice-cold water I fell into when jumping out of the plane froze all my limbs, making me numb. I was drowning, and I was okay with that. I watched as the muffled world around me slowed down into a glassy blur. I slept all day, I didn't eat, I wasn't present, I was worthless. That went on for months. Just when I thought I made it out of a low, I dropped back down again. Alyssa was the one who convinced me to see a therapist. That's why she knew I was lying. Because she knew me better than I knew myself.

Alyssa sighed. She always saw right through me. She had stopped eating, and despite the poor connection, I could see her forehead frowning at me as she furrowed her eyebrows. She looked like a toddler who didn't get money from the tooth fairy, sad and skeptical—maybe it was the sandwich.

"I just want the best for you." We didn't say much after that. She had pointed out the elephant in the room. I shut my laptop and looked outside of my window. There wasn't much of a view, just dead grass, and a crumbling brick wall. *How did I get stuck with the one shitty view in this entire school?* I leaned back in my chair stretching my arms up over my head as I obnoxiously moaned. I stared up at the water-stained ceiling, thinking about what it was like before roommates. Back when I only dealt with my leech of a little sister—okay, she's not that bad.

What *would* my parents say? I hadn't been home since the last debacle. I was too scared. It was on Memorial Day weekend. My family was having a barbeque even though the BBQ machine needed a kick in the rear just to work properly, and even then, we always ended up having to scrape off the burnt parts off the hotdogs and burgers. My mom and sister were sitting in the faded-white splintery lawn chairs with a few of my aunts. My grandfather was standing at the screen door proudly watching the family he had created. A few of my cousins were playing their own version of football with an oversized hacky sack.

I was lying on the grass in front of the veranda of my grandparents' home, dozing in and out of sleep and eavesdropping into the conversations around me about who was getting married, whose boyfriend was a bum, who stole Aunt Cathy's cat...who started therapy. I rolled to my side and spotted my grandmother and my dad on the metal hammock just across the lawn and watched as my grandmother spilled the tea about my cousin, Josh. Well, more like *spit* the tea about him.

"He went to a psychiatrist for *stress*."

"What the fuck? He needs to grow a pair and deal with it like the rest of us. I didn't bitch when I was working in a factory at twelve."

I winced. Where was Josh? I scanned the veranda, and there he was, alone at the farthest edge away from the rest of the family as usual. I pushed myself up and brushed off the damp grass from my rear—I didn't like these pants anyway— and cautiously walked over to Josh.

"Did you think your burger was a piece of charcoal, too?" He smirked a bit. "How are you holding up?" He looked old for someone in his mid-twenties. His hair wasn't combed and stuck out in the wrong places, the bags under his eyes weighing down his pale face, the lines at the sides of his mouth pointing down. He looked ready to cry, but I knew he wouldn't. Josh has always been the oddball in our family. Maybe that's why I was so drawn to him. There was always something to talk about when it came to talking about him. When he dropped out, when he threw Aunt Cathy's phone into a lake—it was always Aunt Cathy—when he got a boyfriend. He was bold, but even he could only take so much backlash. He was getting enough shit already.

Josh looked down at his hands as he fiddled with the button on his flannel. He looked where everyone was as they cheerfully laughed and made the occasional side glance in our direction. He took a sharp breath in and blinked rapidly then gently squeezed my shoulder. I laid my head against his shoulder. "It'll be alright."

"Thank you." Josh hasn't visited the family since then. Who could blame him?

My phone's muffled buzzing snapped me out of my reverie. I pushed aside all the dark clothes and crumbled notes on my bed in desperate search of my phone. Found it.

"Hi, Dad. What's up?"

"What time are you coming?"

"My train leaves at 2:00, so probably around 2:30ish…?"

"Alright, let me know when you are close. Love you."

"I love you too. Dad?" He hung up.

The train was relatively empty for a Friday. Across from me, there was a young lady in blue scrubs with a tight bun on the top of her head. The bags under her eyes made me wonder how hard she works, if she had kids, if she went to school. I like to think she moved out of her parents' home to go to school, which is why she worked so hard—who knows? I could be way off, and she could have been a crackhead for all I knew. A few seats to my left was a tall, lanky man in a business suit who would have been more appealing to look at if it wasn't for the off-centered toupee. I stared a bit too long.

"Excuse me," I apologized sheepishly and looked down at my feet. The floor of the train used to be carpet, but now all I could see was the faded strip marks. My hands found some loose threading on the faded-navy blue cushions and began to fiddle with the string. I looked at the back of my forearm. There were faded scars from where I used to scratch at my arms when I was anxious. I really have come a long way.

"Sam? Sweetie, did you hear me?"

"What?"

"I asked if you've talked to your parents?"

I was stuck in my usual reverie. I was sitting in the familiar loveseat that was a faded lilac, which looked greyer than anything. It really added to the aesthetic of the already dull, ice box labeled "Dr. Riley" also known as an office. The stitching on the stained armrests told many stories from past sessions. It was often my way of distracting myself from picking at my own skin. The walls were covered with self-help posters for drug abuse, suicide awareness, all that cliché inspirational bullshit: "It's okay to not be okay," "Mental health matters," and my personal favorite, "Stamp out stigma." I wondered if those posters ever actually helped anyone.

"Sam, they have a right to know. They are going to find out eventually. Wouldn't it be better if they heard it from you and not a bill in the mail?"

Susan—oops, I mean Dr. Riley—was right. One of the perks of being a youngster is mooching off of my parents' insurance plan. They have always told me to focus on school and worry about the "adult things" later. So, that's what I've done. The closest "adult thing" I've dealt with is probably applying for financial aid, but even then, it was based off my parents' income. I was, and still kind of am, very reliant on my parents. So, when it came down to finding a therapist, I was on my own. It wasn't too difficult if I'm being fully honest here. What was difficult was covering all the possible tracks that could give my parents any hint that I was seeing a therapist. Changing mailing addresses, email addresses, ensuring that my information was restricted to my eyes only. It took a while, but I managed. The only issue was, even though I did everything I could to keep my secret, they were still the head honchos.

"Sam, can you go get the mail?"

Every Saturday morning, my mom religiously cleaned the house with her 80s jams accompanying her in the background. If you were lucky, you could catch her moonwalking when mopping or vacuuming. She was in the kitchen washing the dishes, which was across from the living room. I was lying on our blood-red-leather couch, while my sister sat on the wood floor mindlessly scrolling through Netflix. It was like Russian roulette when it came to my mom choosing who would be her victim to go get the mail. I was the victim that day. I groaned and tried bribing my sister into taking my place, but she's just as lazy as me.

I trudged my way outside to the front yard, head down scrolling through Twitter on my phone. When I reached the rusty mailbox, I didn't fully pay attention until I noticed there was nothing inside. I didn't think much of it, for I figured my dad probably got it. Sure enough, he did. Just as I made my way back inside, my dad shouted for me to come into his office. I peeked my head through his doorway. There was a bunch of fliers on the floor for future Open Houses, a stack of color-coded files on top of his file cabinet. Why use the file cabinet, when the top of it works just fine? His poorly painted black desk had a Kobe Bryant bobble head next to his MacBook across from where I was.

"Did you go to the doctor's recently?"

My heart sunk, my throat tightened up, my body suddenly felt very heavy. It's okay. Just breathe. "Um. What?" He held up a white and blue letter that had my name printed on the front in small black letters, taunting me. *Samantha N. Guisa*. My heart was racing, and I felt a rush of coldness spread throughout my body, starting at my toes and clawing its way up my spine. I reached over quickly to grab the evidence out of his hand before he could investigate further. I fumbled with the letter, attempting to open the piece of shit. I hope he doesn't suspect anything.

"Oh. It's just them reminding me to get a physical. They've been bugging me about that a lot recently. I'll take care of it." Lie.

"Oh. As long as you're okay. Get on that, dork."

I rushed out as quickly as possible, trying to avoid suspicion and read the letter in the bathroom—the one place in the house where I could be alone in private. It was the bill statement.

I didn't like Susan at first. She didn't give me any specific reason to not like her other than preference to have pineapple on pizza. The first couple of sessions I was just being difficult, but in my defense, the conversation dragged on as she asked the same usual questions. We both kind of just went through the motions. It wasn't until she came in late one day soaked from the rain and covered in mud from the knees down and her eye makeup runny.

"Fuck Chicago. I look like a goth Betty Boop."

I don't know why but, in that moment, I found that hilarious. From that point forward, both of our barriers came down. She became my mom away from home. She genuinely wanted the best for me. I don't know how she tolerated my bullshit, but she did. I knew she was right about telling my parents about seeing her—oh wow. This sounds like a relationship problem—and I wanted to make her proud.

"Last stop. Oak Park."

I grabbed my faded green duffel bag and checked the time on my phone. *2:45.* I forgot to text my dad. Oh well. I walked off the train with the toupee guy and tight bun lady close behind me. I waited on a bench insulated with blue rubber near the sign that said, "Pick up." I watched my two companions as they waited for their rides. The man with a toupee left first. A red sedan pulled up to the curb and parked. A short, plump man with skin the color of brass practically ran into the toupee guy's arms and clumsily landed a kiss. They were an odd pair, but they somehow suited each other.

Next up was tight bun lady. A black SUV pulled up soon after toupee guy left with his plump lover. I looked closer, and I noticed tight bun lady's eyes were welling up with tears. I watched an older frail man make his way out to help the young woman with her bag. When she saw him, she broke down and cried into his chest. He held her silently and softly patted the back of her head.

"Sky, it's okay. We'll figure something out." Sky. She looked up at the old man, eyes red and puffy. She looked so young and vulnerable. It oddly suited her. She was a beautiful.

"I love you, Papa."

The two left. It was just me and my anxiety then. I thought about the two strangers. I thought about their interactions with their loved ones. I may not have known them personally, but seeing them vulnerable with their guards down was beautiful to me. Vulnerability often goes unappreciated or unnoticed. It's uncomfortable. It's terrifying. It's intimate. I thought about Josh and his strength despite being the criticized. I thought about Susan, Dr. Riley, and her compassion towards others. I thought about Alyssa and her tenacious attitude towards life. We were all just specks in the universe trying to survive.

My dad pulled up in our silver Honda Accord. My chest instantly tightened as I thought about how I would break the news to my parents. It wasn't really a big deal. Not really. The ride home felt long. My dad asked me questions about school, grades, the standard small talk with a parent. I watched as we passed the old brick buildings, the scattered trees, then there it was. I was home. My dad honked as he pulled up into the driveway, and my sister came out running. As soon as I closed the car door, she rammed me into the car, throwing her arms around me. I'd be lying if I said I didn't miss my family. I felt tears in the back of my throat, easing their way into my eyes. I felt guilty for not visiting them for so long. I quickly blinked the tears away and hugged my sister back.

We made our way inside, and the moment my mom saw me, her face lit up as she jumped up from the couch. The tiny five-foot woman grabbed me in a chokehold and gave me a noogie. Gosh, I loved my family.

Once the excitement of my arrival subsided a bit, my sister retreated back into her room as typical little sisters do. My mom and dad lazed around on the couch, as they continued to watch *Master Chef*. I went inside my room to unpack and unwind. I stared at my neon green walls that were covered in pictures of Alyssa and me, my baby blue record player on my white desk, the stack of books across my dresser. There really is no place like home. I crave to have the closeness I used to have with my family. I'm tired of hiding. It's time.

I took a deep breath and made my way into the living room. I took a moment to watch my parents. I thought about how supportive they have been throughout my life. Why would this change anything? Why would this define our relationship? Why should this define who I am? It doesn't, and it won't.

"Mom?"

"Dad?"

About the Author

Elizabeth Ojeda was raised in Rialto, California, and she is currently a student at the University of California, Irvine, studying Psychology and Social Behavior and Educational Sciences. She currently volunteers as a Karate Assistant at Karate for All, which is a Community Occupational Therapy based Martial Arts Program that was developed specifically for those with special needs. She is also a Crisis Counselor through the Crisis Text Line, where she interacts with those in dire need of a support system. Aside from her volunteer work, Elizabeth enjoys practicing taekwondo, people watching, and spending time with her family. She would like to thank her parents, Angelina, Cynthia, and most importantly, Jorge for their unconditional love and support, for she has no idea what she would do without them.

THE WEAK ARE THE STRONGEST

ISISS PROBY

Weakness

The old beaconed houses held secrets

It kept me up, left me sleepless

The grey sky knows my weakness

My mental thesis

• Su

CHAPTER 1: The Village's Sacrifices

Throughout the entirety of the village, there were many different clans that always migrated. Some ruled, and some eventually faded away to extinction or were conquered by other clans. Some clans and their armies were undefeated; others were just considered weaklings; some were too desperate for power, which made them reckless. Overall, in the near future, these armies and their clans will be conquered. Although the rulers of each clan may not show it, all of them fear and day by day become paranoid for this day to come. In the ancient scroll, when all the clans were united in this year, there were extraordinary baby boys and girls, and they were destined to overthrow each and every ruler.

But, what the ancient scroll did not see was there was a ruler in the shadows, waiting for this day to happen. On this night, all of the mothers, in different villages, miraculously bore children at the same time. The mothers were exhausted and flushed, while the fathers admired or despised the special gift they had brought into the world.

One family, belonging to the Shadows and Winds clan, bore three children, all born on the same day, but there was one that was clearly more developed than the other two. They were born with different hair color, and it was apparent they would have different abilities. Once the babies were born, the unknown ruler sent ninjas to take the babies, but the parents were allowed to give their children items for the babies to cherish and keep. However, they never knew when their child would actually come back home to them.

The mother of the three children handed the ninjas identical necklaces and a picture, while the father planted his quivering lips on each of their foreheads. The mother cried as she held her babies for the last time, while the father only shed a single tear, trying his best to be strong while witnessing the greatest sorrow.

The three gurgling babies were carried away by the unknown men, and they were taken to the underground academy. The academy was hidden from the naked eye; no one could see it unless the ruler allowed them to or they were chosen as well as their family members. No one realized an uprising ruler was taking unordinary babies from different clans to create a powerful army. Then, a family belonging to the Mystical Water Clan bore a baby boy. The father and mother smiled in happiness, but in only a few minutes, their happiness was taken away by the unknown men. The father fought the ninjas, but they were too skilled and unmerciful. They killed the father. The mother's eyes widened with shock, and she wanted to sob, but she had to act strong. The ninjas had to make a decision either to kill her or just to leave, but they decided to leave her to grieve and mourn.

But before they left, she said, "Please let me give something to my baby boy." Although she may have been exhausted but could not let them know, she gave the baby boy a peck and key connected to a beaded bracelet. She tried to touch him for the last time, but the ninja snatched him away from her. As she continued to be heartbroken, she went to her fallen husband and wept. The ninjas evilly smirked at her and walked out off with her son.

Next, in another village, in the Earth and Rain clan, the newborn baby was destined to be an heir to the throne of the small but strong clan but was taken away by the ninjas. The father of the baby boy despised his son's existence because he wanted to be in power. The mother seemed to be the only one who cared for his wellbeing. The father was willing to give him away, while the mother protested, but no one listened to her.

The ninjas took the child and did not ask the mother if she wanted to send him off with anything. The father did not want the baby boy to know he was an heir, so that there be no traces of the village to be seen or heard of. The father also told the guards to make sure the baby boy had no knowledge of his home village at all. His pride and his jealousy led to that horrible decision, and he did not want to give up his throne. At that moment, the mother began to lose her love for her husband and the respect she had from him.

None of the families knew what was going on with their kids until fifteen years later. The academy had sent each family a picture of their child to give them a sense of comfort and closure. Fifteen years later, the stolen children were doing a strenuous obstacle course, and no one questioned why. Each of the teens were exhausted, but they were driven and kept going because they knew if they didn't there would be punishment and dire circumstances for not completing the task. All of sudden, one of them finally wondered why they were there and how they got there. I wondered a lot of things but did not dare to speak up, even though I knew of my mother and father.

I was the oldest of the triplets because I was born first with purple hair, and now that I am a teen, my hair went from thin, short and straight to very spiky that was past my shoulder blades. All of a sudden, I heard, "Mizuki, focus," my sensei yelled, and I continued the course. After our obstacle course, we ate lunch for brief period of time.

Today, I decided to emerge in the moment as I looked around and noticed there were many kids in this academy. I was interrupted by my sisters who were sitting next to me at a table, asking me if we were able to see Mom and Dad again. I only shut down their curiosity and optimism with the realization that the only chance we had was to rise up in the ranks to be approved for field assignments.

The alarm rang and the speaker rang through the room to remind us that it is "combat time," and we had to go to our class by ages. We went into the battle room and knelt down ready to see the first fight of the day. The sensei called two students, one named Aidan Kuzumaki and another kid in our class. Once the sensei gave Aidan the blindfold, everything was going to change...

TO BE CONTINUED: SEPTEMBER 2018 –

WHEN THE COMPLETE NOVEL RELEASES!!!

About the Author

Isiss Proby is currently a college student, who is driven to continue to write more stories. Also, her current book is in the works for September of this year.

Interlaced

Jessica Yslas

"This life is what you make it. No matter what, you're going to mess up sometimes, it's a universal truth. But the good part is you get to decide how you're going to mess it up. Girls will be your friends - they'll act like it anyway. But just remember, some come, some go. The ones that stay with you through everything - they're your true best friends. Don't let go of them. Also remember, sisters make the best friends in the world. As for lovers, well, they'll come and go too. And baby, I hate to say it, most of them - actually pretty much all of them are going to break your heart, but you can't give up because if you give up, you'll never find your soulmate. You'll never find that half who makes you whole and that goes for everything. Just because you fail once, doesn't mean you're gonna fail at everything. Keep trying, hold on, and always, always, always believe in yourself, because if you don't, then who will, sweetie? So keep your head high, keep your chin up, and most importantly, keep smiling, because life's a beautiful thing and there's so much to smile about."

— Marilyn Monroe

I felt the warmth radiating from his lips that traced the side of my neck. His hands intertwined with mine gave me the feeling of bliss. Sparks flew as our lips met. My hands left his to interlace my hands into his hair. His short black locks smoothly laced around my fingers in an instant. The smell of his skin surrounded me like incense of the woods during the summer. That is the smell that only comes from being in the sun for many hours on end. The muscles pressed against my stomach sent chills down my back. His muscular legs pressed against my legs and mine against his was very exhilarating, and I almost blacked out. He grabbed my hips and rubbed his long and erect partner against my inner thigh.

Then sinking lower, he placed butterfly kisses along my neck. When he reached my breasts, he gathered my right one in his mouth and sucked it. As he eased off it, he flicked his tongue over the nipple. I moaned out of pleasure. As he moved to my left breast, I did not notice his hand slip lower until he touched my mound. He slipped one finger inside of me while sucking on my breast. He started to pulse it in and out. Then, he added another finger. At that moment, he bit the nipple. Slowly, his head slipped lower until his head was between my legs. I could not look at him.

Then, out of nowhere, he said, "Look at me savor you." My eyes shot open as he licked my bud and nibbled on it. My hand intertwined with his hair as he drove his tongue in and out in a pattern. Then, he pulled his tongue out and whispered, "Just like honey." Slowly, he crept up and placed his partner at the entrance of my flower and slowly proceeded to enter.

As he reached my hymen, he stopped and placed his head next to mine and whispered, "This will only hurt a little bit." All I could do was nod my head yes. He quickly pulled back out a little then quickly slammed right back in. I screamed out in pain; then, just as fast as it happened, it dissipated as he held still within me. As soon as I relaxed, he slowly started to move. Then, he started to get faster as I moaned out in joy. He slowly pulled out and laid next to me and whispered, "I love you, Aphrodite." He gathered me in his arms. As he did, we lay together. He placed his hands on mine. The touch of his strong gentle hands caressing my hips up and down sent chills through my body. He then turned me to face him as he pressed his lips against mine. It gave my heart a little leap of joy. I was ready for more, and so was he.

Damn, his skin sent shock waves of ecstasy through my body. His lips neared my ear as he whispered, "You will always be mine and nobody else's. I will always fight for you even if it costs me my life. Don't you ever forget that my love." He slightly nibbled on my ear as I jolted out of bliss and pulled him closer into my arms. The muscles on his back moved when I touched his upper back; he shivered from my touch. He whispered in my ear quite sexily, "Only you can make me feel this way. No one else has the power to do this. You should know that I only long for your touch and any one that gets in the way might get hurt." I quickly pulled him closer and whispered in his ear, "I never will forget that but understand that I won't let anyone get as close to you as I am." A smile spread across his face giving my heart a bit of excitement and causing my body to want to touch his more than ever before. I felt so connected to him in every way that my body had always yearned for a feeling, for that emotion.

As my mind blurred from the touch of him, I heard a siren in the background and pleaded it to end. Though the sound only got louder as it got closer, and in shock when the sound was at my ear, I was out of bed in an instant.

I realized that it was the same dream that I have every night with the man I did not know. It has always been the same dream for three years now. I have grown accustomed to seeing him in my dreams. His plush lips, caramel skin, with black hair, with those sky blue eyes that capture my heart as I look at him. Dreams never do come true, or so I thought. Oh, and my name is Aphrodite Adonia.

This was how every day started out for me, so I had decided it was time to do what I normally did in the morning. I got up and walked to my bathroom to look at myself in the mirror and decided that it was time to get ready. I turned on the water and splashed my face clearing my mind of any doubts that I had about myself. I slip out of my silky pajamas and walk to the shower to turn it on. As I do so, it occurs to me that my parents did not to bother to wake me up yet again. So that meant either I was up before them or I was late, but the time on my clock showed that I was up long before them.

So, I decided to take it slow and steady. I washed my hair with my pomegranate shampoo and conditioned it with my coconut conditioner. The reason why I chose those two smells is that they blend together to create his smell. I did it so if I was sad at school or something, I could smell my hair and think of him. I know it sounds weird and all, but it relaxes me when I get even the slightest scent of him.

Later, after a long walk to school and three gruesome class periods, I ended up in my favorite class, chemistry, and in that class was my best friend Kim Eira. That day, we got to work in groups for the lab though labs are usually worked in groups of three. We only had two since our other member went to a continuation school because he was so far behind. The labs seemed to be taking longer than they usually did for us to finish them though we finished the lab before anyone else in class.

So, Kim and I decided to talk though every time we did, she would always ask about my dreams. Even though she would ask, I would turn the conversation back to her and ask her what her dream had been that night. In the middle of our conversation, our sensei came in with a new student and asked everyone to stop what they were doing, so he could introduce him to the entire class.

I did not look up until he said the new kid's name, which happened to be Dmitri Knight. When I did looked up, my jaw dropped. Just the thought of saying his name felt as if it would just roll off my lips. In the middle of my thoughts, my gaze traveled from his luscious lips to his memorizing eyes. That is when both of our eyes widened though his not as much as mine did. To my side, I heard my friend whisper in my ear, "Wow! What is wrong with you? You look as if you've seen a ghost or are you just into him, because I can see why. He is so damn fine."

Out of the corner of my eye, I saw my friend with the biggest grin I have ever seen her have before. I looked back to the front to be gazed upon by eyes that were making my heart melt in an instant. In my defense, it was because I was

126

staring into the eyes of the man I have dreamed of for three years. I was so entranced that I did not even hear sensei call me.

As I came back into reality, I heard the sensei say, "Aphrodite, did you hear me?" All I could say was, "I'm sorry, sir. I did not hear you. Could you repeat it please?" Doctor Nelson sadly shook his head and said, "Well, Aphrodite, maybe you should listen more often, so that I would not have to repeat things, but you know what I will repeat this only one time, so you are sure to listen to what I say. Do you understand me, Aphrodite?" All I said was, "Yes, sir. I do."

Dr. Nelson then repeated what he had said earlier, "Aphrodite, you will be showing Dmitri around school and to his classes since most of your classes are the same. Now that we have that settled, Dmitri please go take that empty seat next to her and get out some paper and a pen or pencil." As Dmitri walked towards me, we never lost eye contact. As he came to our seats, he literally sat next to me. In our school, we have the desks that are meant to be two separate desks, but they were selected to stay as one desk in order to save money for the school district and to save room in the classrooms.

As he sat down on his side of the desk, our hands touched slightly as he sat down beside me. As we touched, a shock shot through my body making it so I was even more alert of him next to me.

I could tell that he saw me jump slightly though he did not say a thing for the rest of the period; also, he tried not to even touch me at all, even if it was a slight tap or brush of the arms. For the next few minutes, I zoned out as I did my work.

However, I was cautious of my surrounding, especially since the man I had dreamed of was sitting next to me. As soon as the bell rang, my best friend Kim turned to the both of us and said, "Hey, let's go get lunch. I'm starving."

I looked over at Dmitri Knight and smiled at him while asking, "Would you be all right with that? And, if you want I'll show you around after we eat." He smiled and man did that smile melt my heart when it came upon his face and he said, "Sure, I'd love that."

As we packed up our bags, Kim complained that we were taking too long by saying, "Hurry up. I'm wasting away here. Look, I'm gonna just be skin and bones real soon." As we got up out of our sets, our arms brushed against each other sending a shock wave of heat rushing through my whole body. We both jumped back from each other's touch. I looked and saw by the look on his face that he had felt it as well. As we neared the cafeteria, I asked him if he wanted to come with me to get lunch, not knowing if he had his lunch with him. He said, "Why not? I am kind of hungry."

As we walked towards the lunch line, I put my focus on the floor in front of me. As we entered the cafeteria, every girl in line began to glare at me for being next to him. All of a sudden, I was pushed from behind and started to fall into Dmitri's chest. All he could do was stare in shock at what happened, as he held me in his arms.

"Wow... are you alright?" asked Dmitri.

"Um...yea, but can I ask you something?" I asked.

"Sure, what is it?" responded Dmitri.

Shyly, I asked loud enough so only he could hear what I was going to say, "Can you get your hand off my boob? It is really uncomfortable."

"Oh, my God! I am so sorry. I did not realize I was doing that. I am so sorry!" Panicked, Dmitri quickly removed his hand and put it in his pocket.

Once Dmitri's hand was off my breast, we started to walk again.

At that time, in Dmitri's mind all he could think was, *Holy shipwreck. Her breasts are perfect. They felt so good. I felt as if I were in heaven. They were the perfect size; they fit so nicely in my hands. Oh, shit! Why did I have to walk behind her? Her ass is perfect. I just want to grab her like I do in those dreams and just blow her mind. Crap! I can't think this way or else I will not be able to control myself.*

As Dmitri and I got closer to the check-out stand with our lunch, I felt something rub up against me from behind, but I did not have the guts to turn around to see what it was. As we exited the cafeteria, girls kept staring at us both. Then out of nowhere, Dmitri leaned down to my ear and whispered, "I am sorry, but if you want them to stop staring then I will leave, if that is what you want."

I turned towards him and said, "What? No, don't do that! You would be stampeded by a bunch of girls if I left you alone." His eyes were wide as he stared at me due to my response. We continued on down towards Kim, when all of a sudden Dmitri pulled me into an empty hall and shoved me against a wall. I was stunned by his sudden action. I did not know what to do.

"Look at me, Aphrodite…" was all Dmitri said to me. "I know that you know me and from where we know each other. So, tell me was everything in the dreams real for you as it was for me or was it all a lie?" Before I could even respond his lips collided with my own in which silenced me in a split second. His lips were breathtaking, as we held each other in a desperate attempt to solidify our unspoken feelings for one another. My arms circled around his neck in order to gain better access to his mouth. I pulled his head closer as my tongue swiped across his lips asking for permission to enter. He quickly opened his mouth which let our tongues collide with one another's.

That was the first time I had done that to him. Usually, he was the one to ask entrance- well, at least in our dreams. As we struggled to dominate each other, his hand dipped down to my hips, which shocked me because we were still at school, and I was worried that we would be caught. I slightly pushed against his chest, which caused him to break our kiss. He stared at me with a perplexed face; he was probably wondering why I had done that when it was just getting good.

"Stop, we can't do this here. We will get caught, and we won't be able to see each other for a long time…" I stated this while looking into his chest, because I was afraid that if I had been looking into his eye, we would have just continued from where we had left, before I pushed him away.

"So, we can continue this later when we are alone?' asked Dmitri.

"Yes, we can. Now, let's get back to Kim before she comes looking for us," I stated.

"Too late! I already found you two. So, when were you going to tell me that you two knew each other?" stated Kim, as she stood with her hand on her hips looking very upset with me for not saying anything to her. Stunned, I stood speechless for a few moments, until I felt a hand placed on my hip while pulling me back into Dmitri's chest.

A smile crept on to Kim's mouth as she stated, "So, is this the guy from the dream you told me about? If not, then I am going to be furious with you!"

"Yes, it is him, so please don't say anything to anyone." I replied as a blush crept onto my face. As I said that, I felt a squeeze on my hip and a bump on my lower back.

"Why would I tell anyone? From what you have told me about this dream it mean you are meant to be together or at least that is what I think." She smiled as she told us this. "Now come on you two can make out once you two go home, or wherever you two decide to go after school today. Right now, I am hungry, so let's go eat."

We all laughed as we walked to Kim's and my favorite place to eat lunch. Nobody knows about it except us two … and well now, Dmitri of course. As we walked Dmitri's hand never left my hip.

After school, Dmitri and I walked to my house slowly, while talking about different subjects. We looked like a normal pair of kids that were best friends, but the on looker would never know unless they were one of us what we really were to each other. When we reached my house, I opened the door and yelled, "Mom, I'm home, and I have a friend with me!" Thumps were heard as my mother came running from upstairs towards us wanting to know who I brought by. When she saw Dmitri, she stopped in her tracks and stood there with her mouth open.

My mother slowly walked towards Dmitri and me as she mumbled, "How? I thought your father was with Samantha back in Britain? What are you doing here? Why did they not contact me…your parents knew of the agreement … you guys weren't supposed to meet for another five years. What is going on?" All of a sudden my house phone went off. Nervously, I reached for the phone and answered it saying, "Adonia residence. You are speaking with Aphrodite? How can I help you?"

"Um…Yes, can I speak to your mother sweetie?" said the soft female voice on the other end of the telephone line. For some odd reason, she sounded nervous.

"Sure, one moment….Mom, the phone is for you," I stated as she flung her hand out for the phone.

"Why didn't you tell me you were coming back?" my mother spit out at the phone in anger. "Yea, well guess what…? Now they have to know because they are both here in my living room together! Get you round white ass over here right now, or else I will drag you over here!" My mother yelled as she pressed 'end' on the phone.

Fifteen minutes later, the doorbell rang, and my mother flung the door open so hard that the windows shook in the whole house. My mother was furious, or so I thought. As Dmitri and I look towards the front entrance of the house, my mother was enveloping a woman with dark brown hair and blue eyes in a tight hug, and they were both crying as they held each other.

The other woman pulled back and said, "Sorry for not keeping in contact these past few years. Do you forgive me?"

"Of course, Sammy. I will always forgive you for anything you do or don't do!" My weeping mother stated. Dmitri slowly walked forward and said, "Mom, what is going on?"

"Oh, honey. I need you and Aphrodite to sit down. It is a long story, and well... never mind, we are going to sum it up really quick for you two... Well, you two are actually supposed to..." She was cut off before she could finish what she was going to say to us as a man barged in saying, "Love, don't tell them anything. We must let them get to know each other, and on their own, we must let their love blossom."

Without even trying, I knew what to say. "Mom, you don't have to worry. We already know because, we have been in contact for the past three years." As I looked around the room, I saw all the parents' mouths wide open in shock.

"WHAT!!!!!!!" shouted all our parents in unison; it was so loud that I thought that my ear drums would break. Then, Dmitri's hand intertwined with my own as we stood before them, and he let me talk how we sort of already knew about what was going on between our families. Okay, so we lied... Oh, well. I guess we will find out soon or later. I hope for sooner.

As we stood with our back to the wall, I saw Dmitri look at me from the corner of his eye as our parents discussed what we had told them. I feared that they would separate us, and as if Dmitri was reading my mind, he squeezed my hand, as if trying to let me know that he was there for me even if everything went south from there on out.

Only the future would tell what was in store for us, and I didn't mind waiting as long as he was next to me, so we could face it together. This was most definitely going to be the hardest journey I would take in my life- that was just based off the look on all of our parents' faces.

Aphrodite and Dmitri will be back for a second time where they will learn what is to become of them and their love. Is it forbidden or is it what they hope it can and will be?

About the Author

Jessica Yslas is a young woman who was born and raised in La Quinta, California. She has been published once before by CLF Publishing, LLC. She loves to read supernatural romances, which inspire her to write her own stories that were supernatural romances. She will be continuing her previous story from *The Love Mosaic* called "Interlaced" in *The Love Mosaic II* that will be released next year.

What Could Be

From Pinterest

Vanessa Zavala

Young Love

You say you love me
you say you care
But when you look into my eyes
I see and feel something more
I see your soul and you see mine
I feel your love, love words can't describe
You are the one, the one I'll always love
and the one that will always care.... my first love

By Casmine

Once there was a young man named Joey B. who had a girlfriend named Victoria E. Joey and Victoria had many differences and often cheated on each other, but they ended up working through those issues. They were together for about five years. They dated throughout their high school years and during some of their college years. One day, Joey thought, *Maybe it's time to go to the next step of the relationship.*

So, he went up to Victoria and asked her to marry him. She said, "Oh, my goodness. Yes, baby. I love you." They were engaged throughout the college years they spent together. Soon afterward, Victoria completed her classes and was ready to transfer schools- to an out-of-state school. So, they broke up because neither of them believed in long distance relationships. Plus, Joey was already planning to go to Japan. Although they broke up, they still kept in touch for a while. Finally, they stopped communicating.

Meanwhile, there was another girl who coincidentally was named Victoria as well, but her last name was Beltran. She was an outgoing person and was going out with a guy named Joey S. Joey and she were very much in love as well, although there were things that bugged both of them. And, they were having a hard time fixing them. Joey and Victoria made an amazing couple. They got along very well and had very few disagreements. They went only out for nearly two years. She was very much in "love" as they called it, but he was not the favorite boyfriend in her family at all. So, they decided to break it off but to stay "friends"- whatever that meant.

They decided to keep seeing each other but sadly not put a title to it, and Victoria was happy - to a certain extent. She was happy that they were together although they weren't 'together.' However, she wasn't happy that they couldn't even go out on a date, to the movies or hang out in general. Her mom disliked Joey very strongly and didn't want him near her daughter, which is why they ended up not putting a title to the marvelous relationship they had. Joey knew that it would bring problems to her family, and Victoria would be the one to pay for it. They were great together up until the time she had enough of not knowing what they were and wanting to become official with no sneaking around, without of course, her mother knowing- ergo sneaking around. So, they broke it off again, and she decided that time it was for real and there would be no go backs.

Months passed by with them not being in contact with each other.

****

Now, back to Joey B. He had said he no longer wanted to be in a relationship because he was moving to Japan and did not want to hurt anyone.

It was mid-September, and everyone was in school. Victoria Beltran and Joey B. went to the same school but had never seen each other. One day when Joey B. finally saw her, he thought, *Oh, she's cute and looks lonely. I'll just go up to her.* So, he did. Beltran was in the dining hall and had time to spare and was going to watch her favorite thing: Anime. She was alone as she normally would be during her three-hour break. As she was putting her earphones in, Joey came up to her and said, "Hey, is this seat taken?"

She said, "No," very vaguely and continued putting her earphones in.

But, Joey did not really let her do her own thing; he just kept talking to her. Meanwhile, while everything was happening, the thoughts that came to her mind were, *Why is this random guy talking to me?* and *Oh, my goodness! Can this guy just leave, so I can see Anime already!*

Meanwhile, Joey kept talking. He said, "So, I see you are alone here in the dining hall."

"Oh, yes. I was just about to start watching my Anime," said Beltran. Beltran and Joey hit it off very well. But, Victoria was very hesitant about talking to him because she had seen the guys that hang out in the dining hall, and they were all stuck up or were just very rude to everyone. So, she decided to put him on trial.

With them getting along, talking about Anime, and joking around, Joey decided to ask Victoria for her number. It went something like this, "Hey, um... I am having fun and everything, but I have to go to class!"

Victoria said, "Well, alrighty then. I'll see you later."

He said, "Yea, no problem, but since we met and had fun talking and everything, would you mind if we started texting?"

She said, "No, not at all. Here's my number..."

Then, he said, "Alright, thanks. I'll text you later today."

"Ok," said Victoria.

Later that afternoon, he started texting her. They texted throughout that day while she was in class and while he was on break. Their texting led to Victoria not being able to help but laugh loudly during class. They were very flirtatious with each other for a while.

Then, it was time to go home, but because she didn't have a driver's license or permit, she could not drive, so she left on the bus. Victoria had to take two buses to get home. After getting off the first bus, she had to wait for the other bus to get to the station. When she got off the bus, there is a surprise at the station. There he was sitting down, typing his next text for her, while smiling at his phone while texting.

He then looked up and saw her. He said, "You stalker!"

A bit confused and startled, Victoria said, "What..? No, you're the stalker."

He then noticed a spark between them and started to flirt with her in person. And, she followed. She had a Kinesiology class and Earth Science, so she carried a duffle bag with her every other day. That day, she had her duffle bag, and he offered to help her carry it because she had put her books in there, making it heavy.

She said, "Are you sure? It's heavy."

Joey said, "Dude, it's fine. Don't worry about it."

She said, "Well, alrighty then," and they both laughed.

They rode the next bus together and talked about anything and everything. The most common subject was Anime. They were both so into Anime, and they were happy that they had various things in common. Joey and Victoria had a connection that couldn't be described in words, but it sure felt special. Then, it was time for Victoria to get off at her stop. To her surprise, he was getting off at the same stop. She was so shocked that he was getting off there and that she had never seen him there.

Well, time kept passing. As they were walking down the street, he was still helping her with her duffle bag. But then, SNAP, the duffle bag went straight to the ground. All he did at that point was say, "Oh, my goodness! I am so sorry, Tori!"

At that point, all that was running through her head was, *Wow, he called me Tori, and that's saying something to me because only my closest friends call me that... Interesting.*

"No, it's fine. Don't worry about it. I have to go to my street anyway," said Tori.

When the incident happened, it was after 6:30. It was just starting to get dark. When they were walking to the corner to where they were going to part ways to go home, they stopped, and he handed her the duffle bag. Their hands touched. They had a quiet moment with their hands still touching, which led him to grab her hand. They just stared at each other.

She then said, "I have to go, but thanks for walking with me."

"Yeah, it was my pleasure. Text me when you get home," said Joey.

She said, "Sure, but it will not take me long to get home, so you text me when you get home, letting me know you got there safely."

"Sure, once again it'll be my pleasure. Bye."

"Okay, later."

Within the next few blocks, she started to fangirl about the whole afternoon. She then called her best friend, who happened to be a guy she had met in high school, Mariano. They started talking about what happened that day because for her, it seemed too good to be true. She arrived home with the biggest smile. Once she got home, she received a text saying, "Hey, you home?" and that made her night even better. She didn't know why she was so happy with the guy during the time they were together that day. She was confused because before that day she and Joey had been strangers and didn't know each other and then, it was as though they had known each other for a while.

After that day, Joey started going to the dining hall even more to hang out with Tori. She didn't mind because she was starting to get fond of Joey. Joey thought, *Well, if we get along this great through texts and when hanging out at the dining hall, we might as well hang out outside of school.* That day passed, and he didn't say anything because he was too nervous to bring it up. On the outside, it showed that he had something to say but did not want to come out and say it.

The next day passed, and it was around 6:30AM. She was still dead asleep, and he called her to ask if she needed a ride to class because he was going to class as well. She gladly said, "Yeah, sure, and um, if you don't mind coming for me around 7:20, please?"

"No, of course. I'll see you around 7:20 or so."

"Okay," she said. She got out of bed, turned the shower head on, and showered to start getting ready. After getting out of the shower and putting music on, she got another call from Joey.

He said, "Hey, do you mind if I pick you up and go back to my place really fast. I have to pick up my cousins and take them to school, if you don't mind."

"No, of course not. I'll see you around 7:20."

"Okay, thanks."

"No problem."

"Bye."

Then, she finished getting ready. At around 7:10, she called Joey asking if she needed to be outside. He had said yes, so she went outside and waited for him. He was telling her that he was just leaving his place and that he had barely finished getting ready. So in the end, they both had finished getting ready at the same time. When he got there, driving a minivan, she laughed so much. For every second that they were in that van, he had something random or interesting to say. They could talk for hours but sadly school was only twenty to thirty minutes away. They laughed and laughed and enjoyed each other's company completely.

Tori had met a friend name Daisy. One day, Daisy just went up to Tori and asked if she wanted to sit down and grab lunch with her. So, she did.

Any who, Joey was nervous for the moment when he was about to do something he didn't think he was going to do at all. He went up to Tori, as always, and that time he stopped her from continuing her way to the dining hall's lounge.

He said to her, "Hey, today after our classes, would you like to go over to the mall?"

"Okay, sure!" she said shockingly yet excited. She thought, *Okay this guy is weird but in a very good way.* Joey was relieved and happy, yet nervous.

He then said, "Okay, awesome."

They both continued as if that question didn't happen but in some way it did, which is where Daisy comes in again. Because Daisy was brand new to the school, she didn't know anyone. She wanted to make new friends. So, she then texted Tori, asking, "Hey, where are you? Would you like to eat together again?" Tori did not like to check her phone while she was talking to people, but she saw Daisy's text, and she felt bad considering the facts that were on the table. She texted her back saying, "Hey, I am in the lounge. Come on over. I am with a friend."

"Okay," Daisy responded. Twenty minutes passed by and Daisy arrived. Victoria introduced them to each other, "Daisy, this is Joey, and Joey, this is Daisy."

They both responded, "Nice to meet you."

Daisy sat down, and they all talked while they were on break from their classes. After all of their classes ended for the day, Joey and Tori met up and walked to the mall, which was only a block away from the college. He bought her lunch and even bought her a few things after that, while they were walking around. After a few hours, Tori's mom called because it was getting late, and she was still going to take the bus home.

After the phone call, she told him, "Hey, I actually have to get going now. It's getting late, and my mom is starting to get worried."

He said, "Oh, okay. No worries. Let's go back to campus and I'll drive you there."

"Okay," she said very shyly.

After they got back to the campus, they quickly went back to the lot where the van was parked. Joey drove Victoria home. As they were driving, Joey said, "I wish I could drive you home every day, but I just got lucky today that my dad didn't go into work. But, tomorrow it's back to the bus."

Happily, they went on the bus to school and back home together, for the next couple of weeks. Then, one day it happened to be early when they got to go home. They were on the bus on their way home when Joey asked if Tori wanted to go to GameStop for a little bit. She agreed because right then she didn't want to go home. So, they went to GameStop, hung around and played with the demos that were on display. They had so much fun, and people thought they were dating or together. They laughed when they talked about it after they caught the second bus.

After they got off, he walked her home once again. That time he stayed a while longer, and they started talking about their pasts and their past relationships. Tori really opened up, which was surprising because she really did not do that with just anyone. And, Joey did too. He explained how his life had gone because he was from Tecate, Mexico and what he used to do for a living, which was work in a family company, with his dad and uncles. Within his childhood, he had seen various monstrous things. He had been through a lot, such as his mom wanting to abort him when he was only a few months in the tummy. She was never there for him. After he was born, she had dropped him off at his dad's place. His parents had broken up while Joey was growing inside her.

After Joey told half of his story, he asked about her story. She also had a tough backstory. While he had been dealing with his life, Tori had been going through depression, and it made her not want to be in a place where everyone was so judgmental and so horrible, in other words on Earth. After suffering depression for five almost six years, she decided to go into therapy, and it helped to certain extent. It made her have doubts. She went to therapy twice a month for four months. After that, she decided to take a better route and that was to volunteer at church.

They continued to talk about their past and much more. They were sitting down in her front yard. Eventually, they stood up and leaned over Tori's dad's car, and they started talking about how the sunset was beautiful.

He said, "You're beautiful." She blushed.

He asked her why she didn't have a boyfriend. Tori answered because she wasn't looking for one at the moment. And he asked if she liked someone. Her response was, "Maybe." She returned the question.

He said, "Yes, I do. But I don't know if she likes me because she said she is not looking for anyone." All of a sudden, she started blushing again and didn't say anything. Until he started asking, "What is stopping you from getting a boyfriend?"

She said, "The fact that guys nowadays only want to play around with girls and how the generation is messed up. Nothing really. Plus, it's not like I have guys saying that they like me, so it's whatever. It will happen when it decides to happen."

"That is so true, so tell me something I'd like to know."

"Okay."

"What if there was someone who is interested in you but is scared of what will happen next?"

"Well, whatever happens next will be up to him."

Joey said, "Okay, understood, and do you think that she could be interested in me?"

Her response was, "Well, she could be but have you told her anything?"

"No, I'm scared of what she will say, but I think she already has a clue that it's her," he said.

"Well, let her know and see if she feels the same way," said Tori.

"I think we could work, and we have a lot of things in common, and we get along very well. Tori, you seem to like me too, even Daisy thinks so, so I know this is sudden and we hardly know each other, but we can work through it, hanging out and such, so Tori what do you say, give us a shot? And if it doesn't work out we can still be friends and still hang around at school and stuff."

Victoria was thinking, *Hmm, is this true or am I dreaming? It sure seems like a fairytale that is coming true for me. Who knows? Maybe this guy will actually be serious with me and not mess around with me. Oh, gosh! I am actually happy about this, and I don't know how to respond. But, I don't think he is over his ex-girlfriend because they are still in contact. I don't know if he is over her and most likely he isn't over her, but then again he wouldn't be saying this if he wasn't over her. Hmm...*

His thoughts with everything were, *Oh, my gosh! What did I do? What if she doesn't like me back? She looks very pretty today! No focus! What if she does like someone else? What if it's that one best friend of hers! No, she told me there was nothing there. Okay, maybe I'm overreacting and she does like me and everything is on the right track. Okay, I'll let her think about it for a few minutes.*

After a few minutes, her response was...

About the Author

Vanessa Zavala is nineteen years old, and this is her second time being published. She is a full-time student at College of the Desert, with plans to transfer in Spring of 2017. At her transfer school, which is still undetermined, she is planning to double major in Psychology and in Liberal Arts. She is planning on going into Social Work for Child Protection Services. She is currently actively volunteering at her church. In her free time, she loves to write short stories and poems. She also loves to draw, listen to music, play piano, hang around her family and friends, and being physically active. Vanessa also tries to live every day with a smile.

If Only

Dr. C. White-Elliott

Dedicated to the man in my dreams

In the recesses of her mind, all she could do was think about him. He was in her every waking thought. The thoughts were so strong and consistent that he even found his way into her dreams. That night, as her tired body relaxed and her head reclined against the soft pillow, she felt herself falling into a deep sleep.

Normally, it would take thirty minutes or more before sleep captured her, but that night, in just moments, she was asleep. And just like every other night that week, there he was dressed in a neatly pressed suit. This one was an all-black suit, with a plaid black and gray button-down dress shirt, but no tie. His shoes were shined, with no scuff marks in sight. He stood with his head slightly tilted down, with one hand holding the top of his jacket and the other on the brim of the hat, while being turned slightly in her direction.

As he lifted his head, the look in his eyes said everything he would not allow his mouth to say. She knew he felt the same way about her, even if his pride and ego wouldn't allow him to utter the words. But his gentle touch told her more than she could ever imagine he would feel for her. The times they had shared together had not been lengthy. But in the short amount of time, their feelings had developed- seemingly out of nowhere. Each time they found themselves in each other's presence, it just felt normal and natural, but the reality was- it was far from that.

As he stood there watching her, she began to blush. She felt his eyes passing over every inch of her body. Well, at least the parts he could see. She knew she had chosen the perfect outfit for his appetite. He never said much about her choice of clothing, but one thing she knew for certain - a man is a man. And with the way he was eyeing her and the curves of her hips and the way the dress fit tightly across her breasts, she knew the white summer dress that flowed past her thighs to just above her knees was a hit.

Before she knew it, he was standing right in front of her with his arm around her waist and his hand on the small of her back bringing her body close to his. She could feel the warmth of his breath against her neck.

At that moment, internally her resolve went weak, but her outward composure did not change. One of the mottos she always kept in the back of her mind was, 'Never let them see you sweat.' 'Them,' of course, referred to men.

Although they both knew the feelings they shared were mutual, they both tried desperately not to let them show. He, of course, more than she. She, on the other hand, wanted to be a bit more carefree. But because he was reserved, she was determined to be equally as reserved. Well..... as long as she could hold out.

With his arm around her waist, he looked deeply into her eyes. And, as her eyes met his, he whispered softly, "Kiss me." Without a word, her lips met his, and they shared the most passionate kiss. As he held her even tighter, her arms lifted slowly and circled around his neck. With one hand on the back of his neck, she pulled his head further down to hers as they continued their kiss. The emotions that passed between them were surreal.

As they kissed, thoughts were running rapidly through both of their minds. Silently, they both wondered, *'What if?'* But the reality was *'what if'* was not a remote possibility.

The passion that she felt permeated through her dream to her real self, to the body that lie limp in the bed. The emotions were so strong that they stirred her awake from her deep sleep. She slowly awakened, and her hand slid across the bed to the empty space next to her. *If only he could be here right now,* she thought.

But, of course, he could not- because he was only a figment in her dream.

About the Editor

Dr. Cassundra White-Elliott resides in California with her family, where as an English/Education professor she teaches at various community colleges and universities.

When writing, she writes with the direction of the Holy Spirit, in an effort to share with God's people all that He has for them.

In addition to teaching and writing, Dr. White-Elliott also serves as an evangelistic teacher. She is the founder of International Women's Commission, a ministry that serves the needs of the entire person, by attending to healing the mind, body, soul, and spirit.

Dr. White-Elliott holds a Ph.D. in Education, a Master's in English Composition, and a Bachelor's in Education.

Dr. White-Elliott is also the founder of CLF Publishing, LLC. For publishing, go online to www.clfpublishing.org.

Gift of Salvation

for

Non-Believers

"For all have sinned, and come short of the glory of God."
Romans 3:23

This section was written especially for non-believers, those who have not accepted the gift of salvation. The gift of salvation saves souls from eternal damnation and is a free gift offered by God himself. John 3:16-18 says, *"For God so loved the world, that he gave his only begotten Son, that whosoever believeth in him should not perish, but have everlasting life. For God sent not his Son into the world to condemn the world; but that the world through him might be saved. He that believeth on him is not condemned: but he that believeth not is condemned already, because he hath not believed in the name of the only begotten Son of God."* This section of scripture tells us God's purpose for giving His son Jesus to the world. The world was in a bad condition. The world was overwrought with sin; the people were living for fleshly desires rather than for God's desires.

As a result of the world's conditions, God decided that He would offer the perfect sacrifice that would save the world from being a place where people were lost and had no hope. He decided that His own son could stand in proxy for the sin-filled world, taking all sin upon Himself.

So Jesus came, born of a virgin, to save this dying world. He walked on this earth for 33 ½ years, doing the work of His Heavenly Father. At the appointed time, He died by way of crucifixion upon a cross at Calvary, on Golgatha's hill. He shed his blood and died for you and for me. Because His blood was pure, it paid the penalty for all unrighteousness and gave those who believe in Him direct access to His father's throne.

Scripture tells us in Matthew 27:51 that the veil of the temple was ripped in two from top to bottom, at the moment that Jesus' spirit left His body. As a result of the veil's removal, we are no longer required to have a high priest make intercession for us. We, as the children of the Most High God, are able to approach the throne God for ourselves, and Jesus sits on the right hand of the Father making intercession for us.

But what is even more miraculous than God offering His own son as the perfect sacrifice was the fact that when Jesus was placed in grave clothes and placed in a tomb, He only remained there until the third day. God would not have it that His son would remain in the heart of the earth forever. In order for people to believe in the awesome power of God and His dear son Jesus, a miracle had to be performed. So, on the third day, after Jesus died on the cross, He was resurrected, demonstrating the omnipotence of God. This very act was the act that would cause people to believe in a god that reigns supreme and holds the power of the universe in His very hands, a god that could save them from themselves.

Today, if you are an unbeliever, you can change your destiny. You can change where you will spend your eternity. Our Heavenly Father gives us the freedom of choice about how we want to live our life here on earth and how we want to spend eternity. In Deuteronomy 30:19, God boldly declares, "*I call heaven and earth to record this day against you, that I have set before you life and death, blessing and cursing: therefore choose life, that both thou and thy seed may live.*"

So, dear friend what choice will you make today? Will you spend your eternity with the Creator or will you suffer Hell's eternal flames? Again, the choice is yours. Just as the men aboard the ship who were with Jonah became believers, you too can make a choice to accept the only one and true living God as your god.

If after reading the above passages, you have decided that you want to spend your eternity in Heaven with God, the creator, and His son Jesus, and the Holy Spirit, read through what has affectionately come to be known as the Roman's Road. This is the road to salvation. As you read through the scriptures that comprise the Roman's Road, you will also read the explanation for each scripture so you will have clarity about what you are reading and confessing.

The Roman's Road to Salvation

The road to salvation begins with Romans 3:23 which declares, *"For all have sinned, and come short of the glory of God."* This scripture explains that everyone has come short of God's glory and needs redemption. Then Romans 6:23a states, *"For the wages of sin is death."* Here, we learn that the consequence of living a life of sin is death. Everyone will experience physical death as a result of the sin committed in the garden of Eden, but those who commit themselves to a life of sin will suffer eternal damnation in the lake of fire (Rev. 19).

Continue with the rest of verse 6:23 that says, *"but the gift of God is eternal life through Jesus Christ our Lord."* There is an alternative to suffering eternal damnation. We can accept the gift of salvation by accepting Jesus as our personal lord and savior. Then, Romans 5:8 says, *"But God commendeth his love toward us, in that, while we were yet sinners, Christ died for us."* We are able to receive the gift of salvation because Christ came to earth and shed His blood for us on the cross.

Continue to Romans 10: 9-10 which says, *"That if thou shalt confess with thy mouth the Lord Jesus, and shalt believe in thine heart that God hath raised him from the dead, thou shalt be saved. For with the heart man believeth unto righteousness; and with the mouth confession is made unto salvation."* If we confess with our mouths that Jesus is the son of God, that he came and died for our sins, and that God raised Him from the dead, we will receive salvation.

Finish with Romans 10:13, which states, *"For whosoever shall call upon the name of the Lord shall be saved."* Call upon the name of God by saying these words, **"Lord Jesus, come into my heart and save me Lord. I believe that you are the Son of God who came and died on the cross for my sins. I believe that you rose from the grave. I also believe that you now sit in heaven on the right side of the Father, making intersession for me. I accept you as my Lord and my Savior."**

Now that you have confessed with your mouth that Jesus is the son of God and that He died for our sins and rose from the grave, **YOU ARE NOW SAVED!!!!** You will spend your eternity in heaven.

The next step is very important- you must find a bible-based church that teaches the word of God and confesses the Lord Jesus Christ to be the son of God. Don't delay. Do this immediately. Do not leave yourself open to the enemy. Get connected with the saints of the Most High God and keep yourself covered with the unspotted blood of the lamb.

Here is my prayer for you.

Father God,

I thank you for the opportunity to minister your word to the unsaved, the unchurched, and the uncommitted. Father God, I pray now for the souls who have just received the gift of salvation. Lord Father, they have opened their hearts to you, and I know that you have received them into your kingdom and written their names in the Book of Life. Father God, I pray that you will touch their lives and show yourself mightily before them. Let their eyes be opened by the scales falling off, allowing them to see clearly.

Father God, I even pray for the backslider, those who have turned away from you after receiving the gift of salvation. You said in your word that you desire that none would perish. So Lord, I send your word to them right now praying that they would confess the iniquity in their heart, repent, and turn from their evil ways, so that they may receive a life of abundance. You said in your word in Matthew Chapter 14, that every knee shall bow before you and every tongue will confess that Jesus is Lord.

Father God, I pray now that we all come under subjection to your word and that we will humbly submit our lives to you. I ask all these things in the name of my Lord and Savior Jesus Christ. Amen, Amen, Amen!!!!

I will continue to pray for your success in your walk with God. Remember, this spiritual walk that you are about to embark on will not be an easy walk, but remember, the race is not given to the swift but to those who endure to the end.

Be blessed with heaven's best. I love you!

A Mother's Heart

Edited by: Dr. Cassundra White-Elliott

A Mother's Heart II

Edited by Dr. Cassundra White-Elliott

A
Mother's
Heart
III

Edited by: Dr. Cassundra White-Elliott

The Mosaic

(A Compilation of Short Stories)

Edited by *Dr. C. White-Elliott*

The Mosaic II

Edited by *Dr. C. White-Elliott*

The Mosaic III

Edited by Dr. C. White-Elliott

THE MOSAIC IV

A Compilation of Short Stories

Edited by Dr. Cassundra White-Elliott

The Mosaic V

A COMPILATION OF SHORT STORIES

EDITED BY: DR. CASSUNDRA WHITE-ELLIOTT

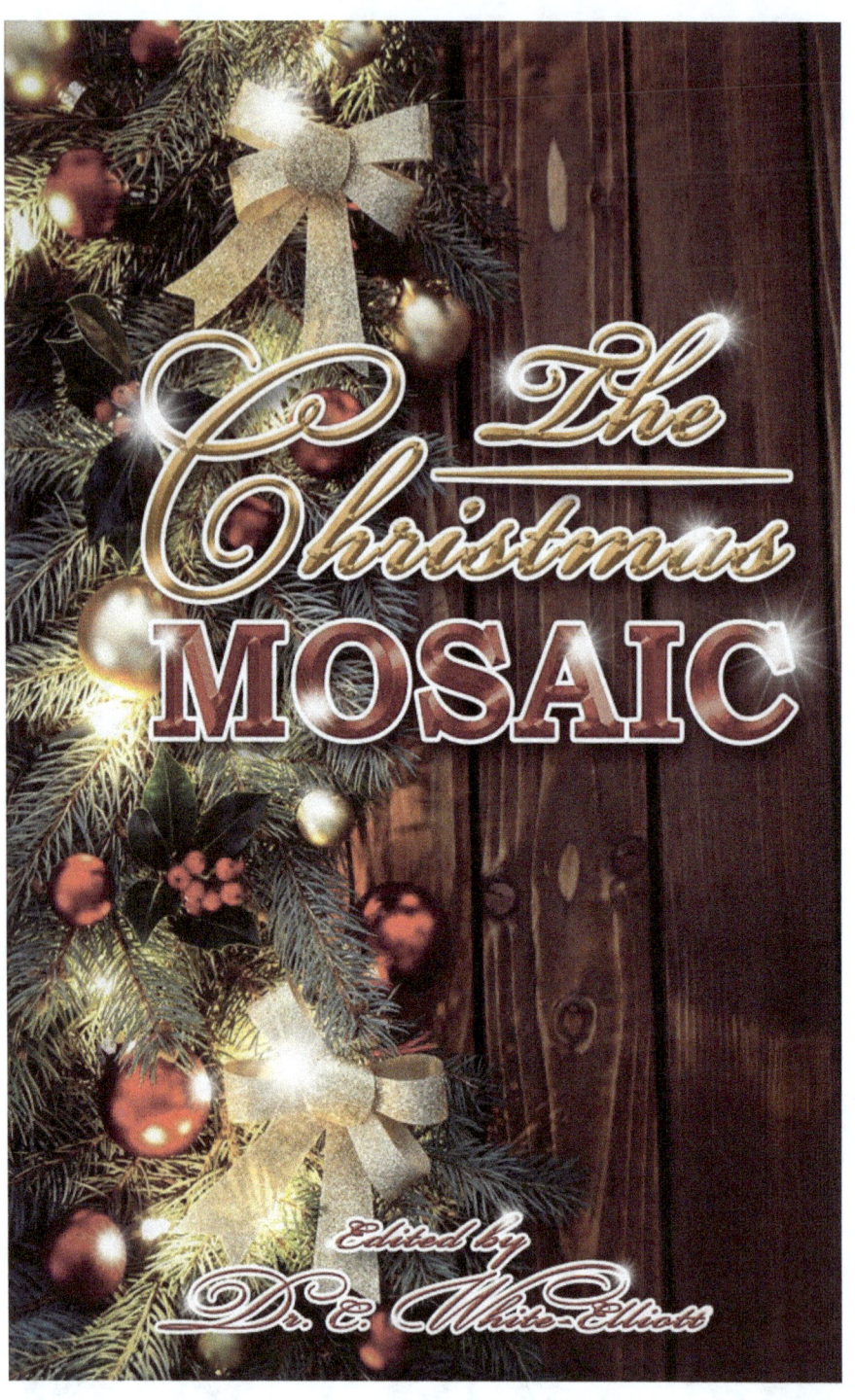

The Christmas MOSAIC

Edited by
Dr. E. White-Elliott

The Christmas
MOSAIC II

Edited by Dr. Cassundra White-Elliott

Edited by *Dr. C. White-Elliott*

All Mosaics and A Mother's Heart compilations can be purchased on amazon.com and barnesandnobles.com. Thank you for your support.